THE SHY ASSASSIN

THE SHY ASSASSIN

A NOVEL

Clara Usón

Translated by Lily Meyer

Vanderbilt University Press
Nashville, Tennessee

LIBRARY OF CONGRESS CATALOGING-IN-PUBLICATION DATA

Names: Usón, Clara, 1961- author | Meyer, Lily translator
Title: The shy assassin : a novel / Clara Usón ; translated by Lily Meyer.

Other titles: Asesino tímido. English
Description: Nashville, Tennessee : Vanderbilt University Press, 2025. | "Originally published in Spanish by Editorial Planeta as El Asesino Tímido."--Title page verso.
Identifiers: LCCN 2025019324 (print) | LCCN 2025019325 (ebook) | ISBN 9780826508317 paperback | ISBN 9780826508324 epub | ISBN 9780826508331 pdf
Subjects: LCGFT: Fiction | Detective and mystery fiction | Novels
Classification: LCC PQ6671.S66 A9413 2025 (print) | LCC PQ6671.S66 (ebook) | DDC 863/.64--dc23/eng/20250620
LC record available at https://lccn.loc.gov/2025019324
LC ebook record available at https://lccn.loc.gov/2025019325

Front cover image: Balcony photographby Pietro Scala/500px via Getty Images

Things are revealed through the memories
we have of them. Remembering a thing
means seeing it—only then—for the first time.

—CESARE PAVESE

CHAPTER 1

I WAS YOUNG at a time when the future seemed young, too, not a sad prolongation of years that dragged on, smelling of dust and trapped air. My contemporaries and I were sure our lives would be better, freer, richer than those of our parents, who we rejected; we were ashamed of them, as if they had decided to live their lives under the dictatorship.

When we're young, we're not afraid of death, or we don't fret about it. Dying strikes the young as a fate so far removed it can't hurt them, only the wan, docile husks—so like the parents they loathe—that time will have turned them into, which is what, if anything, they *do* fear: aging, transforming into adults tied down by routines and responsibilities. No wonder they throw themselves so urgently and passionately into youth, devoting themselves to it, clinging to every last moment of the one stage in life in which newness and choice far outweigh obligation.

I did, anyway; my generation did. We wanted to enjoy ourselves, to be modern (in contrast to our parents, those children of Franco, who we called our *olds*) to try it all, to be European!, and no, we weren't afraid of death, we thought our youth made us invulnerable, but in the end life surprised us, mixing our friends' funerals in with our grandparents.

Life's meaning, if it has one, is a subject that philosophers, theologians, and even poets have been explaining for millennia, along with the reasons we should seek that meaning in transcendence or divinity. Ordinary mortals are too consumed by life's work—jobs, meals, sleep, raising children, paying bills—to have time or desire to reflect on its meaning. If asked, they would say the meaning of life is survival. Why survive? the philosophers, theologians, and poets want to know, but the question goes without reply.

An adolescent has no doubt—or I didn't, when I was one—that the meaning of life is capital-L Love, and her certainty is a good thing; if, as an adolescent, I had intuited or suspected that in adulthood, what would keep me awake at night would be not heartbreak, but money troubles or issues at work, I might have lost my will to live.

By twelve, I'd fallen in love more than fifteen times. My romances were huge, earth-shattering, much more devastating and intense than any of the ones that came later. All the men were perfect, being imaginary, and since I saw no need for messy breakups, we always ended things on good terms. My family often skied at Formigal, driving there in my dad's secondhand Seat 1430, a yellow beater with a much-repaired engine that shivered with fear when my father tried to pass another car. We always began those trips in the dark, rarely getting out the door before 8:00, 9:00, 10:00 at night. My four siblings and I rode in back, between the trunk packed with gear and our parents in the front with their cigarettes, pervading the car with smoke that put my younger brothers to sleep and gave me cover to dream of my love, the ski instructor. He was twenty-six, but the difference in our ages meant as little to me as his girlfriend, a lanky, gorgeous blonde who I liked, but was ready to sacrifice without remorse at the altar of our passion. She'd understand that the ski instructor and I couldn't live without each other; we were each other's destiny. How we looked at each other! We used our eyes to say what language could not. Any good love story has its share of suffering, and we constantly had to confront obstacles that seemed insuperable, but love, in the end, conquered all. Naturally, there were misunderstandings and painful ruptures, times I thought he no longer loved me or when he was the one who lost faith. How we suffered! How my heart pounded under my ski jacket when I ran into him at the store! But I played it cool and was rewarded with sweet reconciliations. I delighted in his cracking voice as he said, teary-eyed, I can't live without you, Clara, you're the love of my life, and my father announced, "We need to get gas."

My siblings and I tumbled out of the car, sleepy and shivering in the winter night. We made many of those stops, usually at highway rest areas, or else rural bars where my dad could have a coffee and a Cuba Libre to wake himself up while my mother drank whisky or a gin and tonic and we children sat and waited to get back in the car, where I broke up with my ski instructor again. (I had no choice. Otherwise, the story led to marriage, which would mean a wedding night, and my Francoist education made it impossible for me to imagine sex. My mother had explained the basics of human reproduction, including coitus, but I understood it only in theory and preferred ruining my idyllic romance to reaching the bridal suite and confessing that I had no idea what to do, which meant my relationship with the ski instructor was doomed.) My father fortified himself against the empty highways and ungodly hours with caffeine, rum and Cokes, and music turned up loud enough to invade my dreams. His songs weren't the soundtrack I would have chosen, but my father was a tape-deck dictator. He had a modern cassette player that restarted automatically but didn't flip or switch tapes, which meant we sometimes listened to one side of an album ten times in a single drive. His tastes ran to rancheras, or else Nati Mistral, María Dolores Pradera, Mercedes Sosa, Joan Baez, Paco Ibáñez, and Georges Moustaki, artists whose repertoires I knew by heart. "Devuélveme el rosario de mi madre," sang María Dolores Pradera, "y quédate con todo lo demás": give me back my mother's rosary, and you can keep all the rest. My ski instructor herded sheep in the summer, and I imagined him in a green meadow, all lambs and wildflowers, leaning on his crook, overwhelmed by his grief at losing me; it just so happened that I was roaming the very same mountain, gathering blossoms for a bouquet, as women in love always do in the country, and I happened to look up and see him. He saw me too, and the car swerved.

"Luis, you're falling asleep!" my mother said as the car swerved. "Do you want me to drive?"

My shepherd and I stared hungrily at each other, neither of us able to move. My dad muttered, "No, I'm okay."

"Maybe you didn't notice," my mom snapped, "but we're in the middle of the highway." My dad wrenched the car into its lane, which made my sleeping brother flop against me; annoyed, I demanded that the shepherd give me back my mother's rosary, and my real mother told my dad, "We should stop before you fall asleep again." Our journey was never going to end.

At that age, I'd read a lot of romance novels. I used to borrow them from the corner store. My favorite storyline was poor girl (a maid, let's say) falls for rich boy (maybe an architect). Initially, his parents opposed the marriage, but she'd win them over, and then someone would reveal that she was secretly from a wealthy family. At the end, wedding bells would ring, and off I'd run to get another book. Even before that, when I was six or seven and couldn't yet read myself anything without pictures, our babysitter entertained us with love stories. Andrés, the youngest, wasn't born yet, and Miguel, the second-youngest, was a baby, so her audience was me, my brother Pablo, and my sister Blanca. I don't remember Pablo paying much attention, but Blanca and I were entranced, though our babysitter always told the same story: once upon a time, in a faraway land, Pablo married a princess and became king. Blanca wed the crown prince of the country next door, which meant she, too, was in line for a throne. I always got the prince's younger brother, which meant contenting myself with being a princess—and I was not content. Who would be? Who'd pick the spare over the heir? In my imagination, I rectified this injustice. I stole my sister's boyfriend and got to be queen.

Sandra Mozarowsky was never a queen. She was never a king's girlfriend. She was the king's lover, though, if you believe the rumors that circulate on the internet and pop up in the occasional book.

As the Franco regime approached death, its subjects started demanding freedom of expression. Not the whole country, but enough of us to be heard. Our demands for liberty got louder and more insistent, and the regime took them to mean that we wanted to see breasts, that we wanted naked women, or half-naked, and so we spent the mid-seventies gaping in awe as our country attained the dubious freedom of a national cinema starring girls who, without fail, opened or removed their tops within seconds of appearing onscreen. Yes, at that moment in Spain, freedom was looking at breasts, and maybe a glimpse of crotch in a semi-legal softcore magazine, though never, ever a penis. Visible male genitalia would be libertinism, which was anathema. According to the many government ministers and functionaries assigned to disseminate this message, liberty was one thing, libertinism another, and it was important that we as a nation not get them confused while we sat and waited for Franco to die. Some of us were eager and excited; some were fretful and afraid; some staged strikes and demonstrations against him and were met with ferocious police repression; in his sickbed, Franco signed his last death sentences with a shaky yet decisive hand; and all the rest of us sat and watched *destape*.

Destape, which means "undressing," was the name we gave our new erotica. We were such innocents, or such pigs, that we really did assume all those tits meant democracy and freedom, or, at the very least, an uplifting promise of both.

Sandra Mozarowsky was a *destape* actress, but before that, she was a girl. She was one her whole life, really: she died at eighteen. She was born in Tangiers in 1958 (three years before me), the third and youngest child of a Russian father, Boris, and Spanish mother, Charo Ruiz de Frías. In 1961 the family moved to Madrid, where Sandra studied at the British School and, according to a piece in the October 1st, 1977, issue of *¡Hola!*, "began to demonstrate her artistic gifts, especially in dance, distinguishing herself as an outstanding ballet student."

(I, too, studied ballet as a girl. For six years, I distinguished myself as the worst dancer in the school's history, according to my teacher, anyway. She made me repeat Beginner six times, hoping in vain my parents would get the message that I wasn't the next Maya Plisetskaya. Every year, I begged my father to let me quit; every year, he refused. My teacher and I were trapped, united by mutual hatred, until a miracle came to pass: she announced to her boss that it was her or me, and, luckily, the head of the dance school chose her. I got expelled, and was spared ballet after that.)

At ten, Sandra made her screen debut in *El otro árbol de Guernica*, which, she explained in an interview, was just luck: a friend of her mother's happened to mention her to the director, Pedro Lazaga. She waited only four years to "get back in front of the camera," as she put it, in *Lo verde empieza en los Pirineos*, which stars José Luis López Vázquez as a Spanish hick with a major issue: any time he meets a girl he likes, he involuntarily tanks the attraction by imagining her with a beard. He goes to a psychologist, who unearths a childhood trauma that caused his compulsive inhibition with women, then reminds him that men are the kings of creation, women their lesser helpmeets.

"From now on," the shrink instructs, "before you go up to a girl, repeat to yourself, 'She's inferior to me.'"

López Vázquez and his buddies plan a trip to Biarritz to see sexy movies, like *Last Tango in Paris*. Pre-*destape*, when anything horny was banned in Spain, our columnists and talking heads hotly debated the line separating erotica from porn. On the one hand, it was a major controversy, but on the other, we all knew erotica was tasteful, it was art, and porn was neither. Regardless, you couldn't see either in Spain. Nudity was a no-go, and so we poured into Biarritz and Perpignan on the weekends to see everything the Generalissimo, in his wisdom, had chosen to censor. Heading home, we felt very free and sophisticated. We'd seen nipples! Pubic hair, too, and a silhouetted hard-on. We'd even seen half a ball.

I say "we" because I, too, went to Perpignan to watch porn. I have no memory of who drove, who else was there. Grown-ups, presumably. I was fourteen, and all I remember is that *Emmanuelle* was sold out and we had to content ourselves with some strange movie, nearly all sex, that nearly bored me to tears. I only refrained from napping because my true goal wasn't just seeing the movie but describing it—i.e., bragging—to my friends.

Before heading to Biarritz, López Vázquez's buddies say goodbye to their miniskirted girlfriends—young and busty, like the rest of the female cast—lying about their destination. After retrieving their third Musketeer, they drive off, singing happily, "¡Tenemos un defecto, que nos gustan las gachís! ¡A la bi, a la ba, a la bim-bom-ba, España, España, y nadie más!" (From title sequence to credits, the movie is an ode to Spanish crudeness. Its heroes are delighted with their own piggishness, their total lack of culture.) When they arrive, they discover that Biarritz is swarming with Spaniards: Not a single car has French plates, and Spanish buses idle en masse outside the theaters. All of Spain has descended on Biarritz to watch what we used to call blue movies, which, of course, delights our heroes, especially since, as good Spaniards, they've never bothered learning any language but their own. (In this vision of the French coast, even the hotel staff is Spanish. Nadiuska, one of Sandra's contemporaries and frequent co-stars, appears, despite her

Polish, French, and German heritage, as a maid from Aragón.)

In one shot, the friends climb up the path that ascends from the beach. Behind them is the ocean, swimmers everywhere, umbrellas on the sand, and I suddenly get the impression that we're there, too; that my mother, siblings, and I will appear any second, my mom weighed down with beach gear: pails, shovels, blow-up toys, a rubber raft. She'll be in an awful mood, a cigarette dangling from her mouth, one of my brothers hanging from her neck, another one clutching her hand, the rest of us shoving each other or shouting about something, excited and hungry and tired from our day at the beach, impervious to my mother telling us to shut up. Yes, we're there, never mind that I've never set foot in Biarritz. We always went to the Mediterranean in the summers. But that light, that streaky, dirty yellow light speckled with holes in the VHS tape, catapults me into my childhood, just like the movie's muscle cars and its men in bell-bottoms and shirts open to the navel, bulges and chest hair on proud display.

Post-beach, our three hicks shut themselves up in a theater, watching the same movie on repeat, gaping at every nipple and thigh. Sandra appears very briefly, as a "young French girl"—her character doesn't merit a name—who sits with our protagonists at the cabaret they go to after finally staggering out of the theater. She and her two friends are cute and young, the Spaniards old and ugly, but the girls still want to sleep with them. (Unsurprising in this version of reality, which holds that Spanish men are irresistible and French women are sluts.) Sandra, lucky girl, gets López Vázquez, who could be not just her dad but her grandfather, but in this movie, as in my fantasies, age differences are irrelevant. She gives him her most charming smiles, her most seductive green-eyed looks, but when he tries to kiss her, the curse strikes. A huge, dark beard sprouts from her face, and he recoils in fear. After that, a showgirl hauls him on stage—in drag? In a duck costume? I can't remember; I turned the movie off as soon as Sandra's scene ended, since I was only watching for her.

When she was sixteen, in 1974, she made her horror debut in *El mariscal del infierno*, starring Paul Naschy (born Jacinto Molina Álvarez) as a villain based on the medieval serial killer Gilles de Rais. Sandra plays a nameless virgin who he sacrifices so he can give her blood to an alchemist who's promised to use it to make him a sorcerer's stone. Sandra's character has no lines, which happened to her so often that she picked up the same techniques as a silent film star. In this role, she's tending crops when Paul Naschy's henchmen kidnap her and drag her into his lair, where she cowers in her white blouse, screaming in fear as the monstrous knight, preparing to rape her, rubs himself against her, rips her top, grabs her breasts. She faints at precisely the right moment and wakes in a canopy bed with Paul Naschy thrashing on the ground beside it, having an epileptic seizure (Sandra, terrified, screams some more). In the next scene, we're outside the castle, and Sandra, gagged and shrouded in red, lies bound on an altar, waiting for the knight's wife, a harpy with painfully overplucked eyebrows, to slit her throat. Our villainess is wearing a strange dress, long and narrow, with an enormous collar and swinging sleeves, paired with a little conical hat like stewardesses wore back then, which creates a hippie-medieval look somewhere between pop and kitsch. She does indeed slit Sandra's throat, and Sandra writhes while it happens, huge breasts bouncing. She's silenced by the gag, but panic transforms her face as it did in nearly all her roles: Sandra as sacrificial lamb, damsel in distress, tied up and murdered by one monster after the next.

Sandra Mozarowsky was beautiful. She had a Slavic face: huge green eyes that tipped up at the corners; wide, plush mouth; pale skin; so much straight, shiny chestnut hair she could have starred in shampoo commercials. *Would* have, if she hadn't died too young to get truly famous. In an old issue of *Pronto*, I saw her described as a "girl-woman who broadcasts sexiness and innocence at the same time . . . green eyes, perfect features, and a statuesque body—though she'll have to be careful not to get fat," which was an exaggeration. Sandra wasn't thin, and she gained weight easily, but given her age, beauty, and willingness to remove her clothes when a script called for it—which was always, every time—no one cared about weight but Sandra herself. Dieting was one of the obsessions of her short life. She's half-naked in many of the photos I've seen of her. In one, her hair spills over her breasts, covering them, as if she were Lady Godiva. In another, she's looking sleepily at the camera, mouth ajar, an embroidered vest just barely covering her nipples. In a third, she's on her knees in a bikini, hands behind her back, pouting suggestively at the camera. And a fourth: Sandra taking (or ripping) her white blouse off, one shoulder already bared. A faint halo seems to encircle her, like a cloud drifting away. She looks, unsettlingly, equal parts virgin and whore.

Sandra made five movies in 1975, the year Franco died. Her characters had names by then, and, even better, some lines. *La noche de las gaviotas* and *El colegio de la muerte* are erotic horror. *Sensualidad*, *Las protegidas* (she's a prostitute in both; if

I'm counting right, she played six sex workers in her abbreviated career) and *Cuando el cuerno suena* (erotic comedy) are pure *destape*.

She was the daughter of a diplomat. In an interview that came out in *Primera Plana* after she died, Sandra swears, or the interviewer makes her swear, that her Russian-born father "got Yugoslavian citizenship for political reasons. During World War II, he went to Cairo as a Yugoslavian attaché, not a Russian, because Yugoslavia wasn't communist back then." In the photos of her funeral, Boris Mozarowsky, her father, stands behind the Orthodox priest, looking like a Soviet spy in the Cold War Hollywood imagination: bald, glasses, expressionless face. But evidently he wasn't a communist but a good Russian, a so-called White Russian. According to *¡Hola!*, that's why he sought asylum in Spain.

Sandra came from a conservative, middle-class background, and I doubt that her parents were thrilled about their youngest daughter's burgeoning career as a *destape* star. In the *Primera Plana* interview, Sandra says, "For four years, my parents were against my acting. Slowly, though, I convinced them to let me do it as long as I could balance it with school." She adds, "My mother gets it now. I'm pretty sure my dad does too, but my mom is my best friend. We talk about everything."

"I already said how much I love my mother," she continues. "I'm also close to my father, but he's a career diplomat. He can't help being cautious and discreet about everything. I mean, he knows I'm his daughter, but he's even cautious about that." (A strange statement, that last one, very hard to interpret. She made several other baffling comments in that interview, including, "I'll only have a child morally, and only if I decide," and,

"My short artistic career has made me reject intimacy with men, though I'm sure there are real men out there. What I'm saying is that I'm a virgin, but only because I haven't found the right guy yet.")

In a short interview she gave the magazine *Diez Minutos* in July 1975 as part of the press tour for *Las protegidas*, her father's supposed opposition to her acting comes up again. Asked if she "connected" to her role as a prostitute, Sandra says, "Well, it's challenging, but I just tried to remember that the character's new to the job, and excited about it."

Her interviewer brings up Ornella Muti, an Italian actress who was a big deal at the time and to whom Sandra was frequently compared, since both had green eyes and feline features. Then he asks, "Has your father changed his tune about your career?"

Sandra's response is equivocal. "He's certainly seen that I can get a lot of parts, one right after the next. I'd say I'm working on a serious, professional level." She comes across as independent, a young woman of character, as she often said of herself in interviews. In July of 1975, Franco wasn't yet dead and Spanish society was Catholic and repressed, and yet Sandra managed to earn a nice living acting in movies that scandalized her family.

In that same issue of *Diez Minutos*, I encounter a distracting story. It's a scoop—*Exclusive!*—titled, "Romeo and Juliet in '75." On the cover, we get a taste: "Meet the lovers whose fate broke Italy's heart! Before throwing themselves under a train, they left us their last words on tape . . ."

Our Juliet, Maria, born in the town of Rapolla, died at seventeen. We don't learn her last name, only that of her Romeo, Michele Gastoni, a nineteen-year-old from nearby

Melfi. Alongside the article are a pair of black-and-white portraits of Juliet (Maria), a sweet, scared-looking girl, and Romeo (Michele) a resolute youth with thin lips and one of the most egregious haircuts I've ever seen, a dense curve of hair clamped over his narrow face. After introducing them, the writer describes the misery and poverty endemic to Basilicata, their home region, perhaps in order to contextualize the appalling tale that comes next. Our two lovers committed suicide by lying on railroad tracks. Every night, the last train arrived in Melfi at 11:45, having passed through the nearby Tunnel of the Seven Bridges at top speed. On the day they died, the teenage couple spent over an hour in the dark tunnel, waiting for the train. During that hour, they—mostly Michele—said goodbye into a tape recorder, preserving their motivations for posterity.

"One, two, three," says Michele. "If you're listening, return this recorder to M— F—. He didn't know why I asked to borrow it. And share this tape with the world. I'm sorry if it upsets people, but it's what I have to do. Life is shit. It's too boring. Maria agrees. Maria, you talk."

"No, no. I don't want to."

"If my parents are listening, and my brother, don't worry. It's not your fault I'm killing myself. It's society. You guys should go on with your lives. Don't remember me. I'm gone, so why bother? Forget me. Maria, seriously, you should talk."

"No."

"Okay," Michele says, and resumes his broadcast, complaining that nobody appreciates him or shares his ideals. He assures the listener that he's not taking the wrong path, and that it's better ("more appropriate," he says) to die than to escape life with drugs and so on. Why should anyone be miserable for sixty or seventy years? he asks, adding that he personally has only been happy for the past seven months, since he met Maria. Then he rejects the idea that suicide is cowardly. "We can leave this life because we know the next one is coming," he says. "I know the next world will be an improvement. Ours is shit! Maria, come on, talk."

Maria's sobbing. "What should I say?" she chokes.

"Say hello to someone. Say goodbye."

"Goodbye to everyone, especially Mama. No, no. I can't."

"Why are you dying?" Michele asks. "What's making you do this?"

"Lots of stuff," says Maria, still crying. "Society, people . . ."

"We want to speak, even though it seems like we don't," says Michele, and launches into a furious denunciation of humanity. He laments not having more opportunities: there are no jobs in his region, but he can't emigrate, since "you can't live without your family"; he'd have gone to university, but he has no money, and apparently never considered working his way through school. He hopes his brother, who "seems happy with his degree and his Army service," will have a good life. He swears that he's never been a self-centered person, no matter what his former classmates might say.

"No one can help me now," he concludes.

"Us," Maria says. "No one can help us."

"Right, right," Michele says. "We're in the same situation. No one can help either of us." He then unleashes a tirade against his sellout dad, who, he says, should stop rolling over and showing his belly to rich men.

Suddenly, Maria interrupts. "I'm ready to talk," she announces, no longer in tears. "I want everyone to know we really thought about this. We were talking about it for a long time, going back and forth, and this morning we made up our minds. We're not changing them now. We're waiting until the train comes, and we're not even going to suffer, really. Not like the idea we had before."

(Her diaries, it seems, referred frequently to a plan to stab each other.) "No one understands us. Society can't understand anyone, which is why we're all prisoners. So don't cry for me, okay? I love you, Mama, Papa. I love my family. I'm cold."

Michele resumes his ranting, hoping he can be an example to others, especially those "who expect Marxism or radical ideas like that to change their lives." He says he and Maria want to be buried together.

"We don't care where," she agrees, "but together."

"All right," he says. "Lights out." We hear them getting ready for the train, Michele saying, "No, no, not here, what if someone sees us? Deeper in the tunnel. Now. Viva love! Viva equality! Viva freedom!"

"Freedom!" Maria echoes. "We're going to be free. In this world, it's never going to happen. We're nobodies. We have no power, no rights, and so we need to go."

Magnanimously, Michele says, "But we don't bear grudges. You don't need to wish for our forgiveness. Just ask Christ. He forgives everyone."

"Hold on!" Maria calls. "Where are you going? You said we'd go together!"

"We're no one," Michele concludes. "But no one else should have to die like this."

After that, the lovers lie quietly in the tunnel. On the tape, we hear the train approaching, their breath, the locomotive whistling into the tunnel, the cars roaring on the tracks, the brakes shrieking, someone shouting, "A shoe!"

"Was it a person?"

"A boy?"

"No, there's a girl here, but she's missing her head."

I'm surprised that a tabloid like *Diez Minutos* would run this story in 1975, alongside "Amparo Muñoz Turns Twenty-One," which features photos of our Señorita Universo blowing out her candles; "Why the Name Pérez Matters"; "Jackie Onassis's Intimate Secrets"; and "In the Sun with Patricia," a color centerfold in which Patricia, who they describe as "Claudia Cardinale meets Candy Rialson, with some Raquel Welch thrown in," poses very seriously in her bikini on a rock by the sea. She's got the same glossy brown mane as Sandra, and, like Sandra, she's not what you'd call thin: actresses and models weren't supposed to be emaciated quite that early in Spain. Oh, and I skipped "Closing Gala at the Opera Festival," which, we learn, was "attended by the Prince and Princess of Spain and their children, Felipe and Cristina." In the photos, a young Princess Sofía appears in a long, vaguely hippie-ish dress, accompanied by her blond children and Prince Juan Carlos, looking tall and handsome in an impeccable dinner jacket.

Diez Minutos' transcript of the taped dialogue has a strange narrative pull. Michele's self-portrait isn't a flattering one. He comes across as a resentful, arrogant, domineering young man, clearly the brains behind both the suicide and the recording, who's not just angry at the world but set on letting everyone know he blames them for his unhappiness. He scolds his parents for their poverty, his brother for his acceptance. He's such an unsympathetic narrator that his death hardly inspires compassion, while his young girlfriend Maria's suicide hurts. She was an innocent, suggestible, infatuated girl, totally willing to submit to her shithead boyfriend. On the tape, she's his echo, so admiring and obedient she let him talk her into suicide. She gave up her life for love. Puppy love, too. She'd only been dating Michele seven months. Surely if he hadn't roped her into this death pact, she'd have dumped him, or he her, leaving her upset, but alive.

How can a seventeen-year-old decide whether life is worth living? How can she reject something she barely knows? I'd like to climb into the tabloid, make my way through that dark tunnel, grab Maria's arm, and drag her away from that creep. "Idiot," I'd say, "can't you tell he doesn't give a shit about you? Let him kill himself if he wants to. You go home to your parents. You're going to get over him, meet someone better—or not! Who cares? But you can't give up your whole life for that jerk. I should know. I'm older than you. I'm experienced," I want to tell Maria, who was born before me and has been dead for forty years.

In his diary, Cesare Pavese wrote, "Suicides are timid murderers. Masochism instead of sadism." He's wrong, though. Suicides seek death. A person who dies by suicide acts with premeditation and malice, like a true killer. Suicide is a killer, a timid one, a shy assassin.

Camus wrote that there is "but one truly serious philosophical problem, and that is suicide. Judging whether life is or is not worth living amounts to answering the fundamental question of philosophy. All the rest—whether or not the world has three dimensions, whether the mind has nine or twelve categories—comes afterward. These are games; one must first answer."

I was taught otherwise in high school. In my philosophy class, the fundamental question we had to answer was: Why is there something rather than nothing? Before answering, we had to break the question down, define something and nothing, ask why we were bothering, why humans need reason, why we search for meanings and destinations rather than assuming life is a projection of the human mind and therefore obeys human logic. Why, why, why, my teacher repeated, and I glanced up from my novel and stopped eating sunflower seeds, my two preferred antidotes to high-school boredom, and listened while she tried her best to explain Leibniz. She was a good teacher, and philosophy was the only subject I liked.

Now, as if Camus were reading over my shoulder, I hear him add, "When did you ever hear about someone dying for an ontological argument? Galileo made an important scientific discovery, but he renounced it outright when his life was in danger. One could argue that he made a good choice. His discovery wasn't worth the pyre. Why should we care whether Earth rotates around the sun or vice versa? What a futile death that would have been.

"But think about how many people die because they decided life was no longer worth living. Think about all the people who let themselves be killed, paradoxically, for the ideas or illusions that give them a reason to live, since what we call a reason to live is also an excellent reason to die. This is why I consider the most pressing question in philosophy to be whether life has a meaning at all."

Chekhov's fiancée, Olga Knipper, once asked him about the meaning of life, and he wrote back, "You ask me what life is? It is like asking what a carrot is. A carrot is a carrot, and nothing more is known." Beckett, similarly, wrote, "What do I know of man's destiny? I could tell you more about radishes." (Maybe Beckett had read Chekhov's answer, and substituted radishes for carrots to seem original.) Ludwig Wittgenstein offered, "I don't know why we are here, but I'm pretty sure it's not to enjoy ourselves." He also wrote, "Whereof one cannot speak, thereof one must remain silent," though Kierkegaard disagreed on that front, writing, "The surest of stubborn silences is not to hold one's tongue but to talk."

Camus devoted an essay, "The Myth of Sisyphus," to the impossible question of suicide. Killing oneself, he writes, is a confession that one cannot keep living, or has no more will to. It means admitting that life's suffering is too great and too pointless. Living, on the other hand, is a habit: "Rising, streetcar, four hours in the office or the factory, meal, streetcar, four hours of work, meal, sleep, and Monday Tuesday Wednesday Thursday Friday and Saturday according to the same rhythm—this path is easily followed most of the time. But one day the 'why' arises and everything begins in that weariness tinged with amazement."

"We live on the future," he writes elsewhere: "'tomorrow,' 'later on,' 'when you have made your way,' 'you will understand when you are old enough.' Such irrelevancies are wonderful, for, after all, it's a matter of dying."

You see, now, the absurdity of the human condition. We live like we have logic and purpose, eagerly anticipating what will happen to us next. We love the idea of tomorrow, when—according to Camus—we should loathe it from the bottom of our hearts, since tomorrow is trying to kill us. We expect an irrational universe to give us meaning, forgetting how indifferent the world is, how unable to answer, how little it cares about us ("I know the next world will be better," said Michele: "this one is shit!").

Understanding absurdity creates a new dilemma: Should we choose death or wait for it?

Camus votes for waiting. He decides we should live as long as possible. We're made of time, nothing else, and we get so little already. Why throw it away? We're not in a rush. Camus says anticipating death is an error. We have no reason to start before the whistle. He says that people who die by suicide delude themselves into believing they've outwitted death—and sickness, misfortune, old age—when really, he argues, suicide means ceding to death. Consenting to it. Abandoning yourself to it. Camus, who died young, sees suicide as submission rather than rebellion; he says the real rebel, the truly free person, is the one who stops caring about the future and serves their time with complete indifference, an argument that doesn't persuade me. In ancient Greece, dying prematurely (like Maria and Michele, or Sandra Mozarowsky) meant you were beloved of the gods, and besides, dragging life out doesn't address the issue of human suffering, or suicide as a way to make that suffering stop.

Camus may not solve the problem of suffering, but he does make it easier to bear. Why should we take our lives seriously if life itself is meaningless and absurd? Seen through his eyes, the absurdity of human existence liberates us from the responsibility of making ourselves useful. Why work toward a future we might not have? Why fret so much about tomorrow when it's going to be just as pointless as today? We may as well relax, ignore our suffering, and launch ourselves into living, as if being on Earth weren't a tragedy but a picaresque, a mounting series of experiences and adventures. Camus says that's better than being like Nietzsche, who lived so intensely, so seriously, that it nearly drove him insane. "'Art and nothing but art,' said Nietzsche. 'We have art in order not to die of the truth.'"

Not so much, says Camus. Creating art is absurd, too. He laughs at the desire to make your mark, to be remembered—an ambition that's really just an illusion. "Art," says Camus, "cannot be the end, the meaning, and the consolation of a life. Creating or not creating changes nothing. The absurd creator does not prize his work. He could repudiate it. He does sometimes repudiate it. An Abyssinia suffices for this, as in the case of Rimbaud."

Camus's argument is lucid, but the liberation it offers is the desolate freedom of an ascetic or a monk. For the rest of us, the only way to survive life's absurdity is to forget it, to take our existence seriously, like children playing seriously with toys. I'd rather wait eagerly for tomorrow than remember that tomorrow will kill me. If the disillusioned life is still absurd, why not live with my illusions? Just as ridiculous, but much less painful. Camus defends himself by claiming that accepting the absurdity of life and then continuing to live is an act of rebellion, but who are we rebelling against? If there's no God, no higher power, then we're just punching the air.

Several months before Sandra Mozarowsky died, an interviewer asked her, "What do you see in your future?"

"I never think about my future. I mean, I can't imagine it. I have a hard time believing in tomorrow."

"What's your goal in life?"

"Being remembered after I die."

"Do you worry about death?"

"Not yet, luckily. I've never experienced it, so I don't know whether we should worry about it or not. I'm a realist, anyway. You're born, you get old, and then you die. It's life. Why should I have a problem with it?"

As far as Sandra was concerned, the meaning of her life was clear. She was going to make her mark, be a hit. I talked to an actor and actress who worked with her on different films, and they agreed: she was a nice girl with good manners, a little shy, very ambitious. She wanted to be a star. I suspect the silly answer she gave the interviewer (whose question was equally silly) hides an unexpected wisdom. A philosophy, even: Since I haven't died, how should I know whether to be afraid of death? She's got a point. What scares us about death is its mystery. Not even the oldest or wisest person can tell us what death is like. Maybe that means we should stop worrying about it so much. In high school, I looked up from my book when my philosophy teacher asked us (herself) about the nature of nothingness because the answer immediately popped into my head: death is nothingness, and nothingness scares us. Religion, in promising life after death, is really just taking pity on our fear, deferring the void, erasing it, denying it to console anyone who believes.

"The real question of life after death isn't whether or not it exists, but even if it does what problem this really solves," declared Wittgenstein, a consummately practical and professional philosopher who shared Sandra Mozarowsky's sensible, dispassionate vision of death. "Death is not an event in life: we do not live to experience death. If we take eternity to mean not infinite temporal duration but timelessness, then eternal life belongs to those who live in the present. Our life has no end in the way in which our visual field has no limits." Death, in other words, has nothing to do with life. It's of another order, and so we shouldn't bother worrying about it. We're in eternity now, we're all eternal—just not forever. We're like tourists, visitors to whom death is strange but fundamentally irrelevant. We don't know what it is and we'll never know what it is, since dying is not-being and we are. A person and his corpse, Wittgenstein says, are about as related as a bird and a rock. So why are we so afraid of the jump?

Virginia Woolf wrote to her lover Vita Sackville-West, "I found myself thinking with intense curiosity about death. Yet if I'm persuaded of anything, it is of mortality—Then why this sense that death is going to be a great excitement?—something positive; active?"

As a child, I envisioned heaven as a swarm of bishops, cardinals, priests, monks, saints, generals, bankers, bankers' wives, and the rest of the rich, an eternal Mass sung by angels and archangels, a dull Francoist eternity I was glad to lose when I understood or realized, around age eleven, that I'd stopped believing in God: not only was I free from the insistent, intrusive eye of that white-bearded old man who watched me even when I was peeing, I was also expelled from his paradise. It was like the day I finally got kicked out of ballet. But after that, inevitably, I had to approach the great mystery, the pit of death. There's nothing humans love like a pit. We may be frightened, but deep down, we're attracted to the void. Stand on the edge of a cliff, and you'll see how positive death suddenly seems. Maybe it's exciting; maybe it'll be a change of pace. Remember, that's how Michele got Maria: life is shitty and cruel to the poor, it sucks for us, so why not give death a shot?

Our fascination with the things we fear is the reason we like horror movies. Sandra starred in seven works of erotic horror: *Los ojos azules de la muñeca rota, El mariscal del infierno, La noche de las gaviotas, El colegio de la muerte, El hombre de los hongos, Beatriz,* and *El espiritista.* She made twenty movies between fourteen and eighteen. (What was I doing at that age? Reading novels and eating sunflower seeds at school, skiing in the winter and lounging on the beach in the summer, reading more novels and eating more sunflower seeds alone in my room. I should be ashamed of myself.)

Camus writes, "The actor's realm is that of the fleeting. Of all kinds of fame, it is known, his is the most ephemeral. At least, this is said in conversation. But all kinds of fame are ephemeral. From the point of view of Sirius, Goethe's works in ten thousand years will be dust and his name forgotten. . . . Of all the glories the least deceptive is the one that is lived." According to Camus, this means actors are lucky. An actor can succeed or not, but if he does, it happens now. He doesn't have to wait for posterity, which is probably never coming. His art means he lives many lives, as many as the characters he plays. He's no one and everyone, pure appearance, so many souls jammed into one body.

So Sandra Mozarowsky chose the best profession, and, as if she sensed that she only had a brief measure of time on Earth, she hardly wasted any of her hours on diversions and distractions. Instead, she worked like a mule, living many lives through her characters. But oh, what lives! Nearly all of them were unbearable.

At sixteen, she got her first starring role, in *El colegio de la muerte*. It's set in Victorian London, but you can tell it was shot in Spain: all the exteriors are in Madrid and Toledo. Sandra plays Leonor, a surprisingly well-nourished orphan. In the opening scene, we see her (of course) mostly naked, tied to the rafters of some sort of dungeon, cowering as one of the mistresses of the orphanage where she lives whips her. After the beating's done, its perpetrator, Miss Colton, bans Sandra from seeing the doctor who's scheduled to visit the next day. Sandra's gorgeous green eyes well with tears: she's secretly in love with the doctor.

Every girl in the orphanage is beautiful, like Sandra, and every single one lives in fear of the vile Miss Colton and her iniquitous boss, Miss Wilkins. Both are desiccated, severe women with overplucked eyebrows, scraped-back hair, and high Victorian collars. From their sly expressions, we know they're the villains. We only get to know one other orphan, Sandra's best friend, played by a very young Victoria Vera. All the other ones vanish—a budget issue, I'm sure. You can tell that the movie (which, to be fair, has its charms) was made on a shoestring. Its whole cast is Spanish, despite the English setting, and Dr. Kruger, the supposed heartthrob, is a gnomelike man with a colossal head. It seems like the sets were borrowed from an amateur theater: one scene takes place in an utterly unrecognizable Regent's Park, which, luckily, is mostly hidden by fog, like a Japanese garden on a fan. Of course, there's a cemetery, a disfigured mad scientist, some interring and disinterring of corpses, some sword fighting, secret tunnels, moonlit escapes, a profoundly homoerotic scene of a lecherous Miss Colton lotioning Sandra's scarred back, white blouse pooling at the young woman's waist. By that point in the story, Sandra's leaving the orphanage—someone has found her a job as a governess—but Miss Colton has a secret to tell her first. Once the blouse is chastely buttoned, the teacher asks Sandra to join her in her room, but Miss Wilkins gets there before Sandra does. Having guessed that the other teacher is about to denounce her, Miss Wilkins stabs Miss Colton with a dagger.

Miss Colton dies after revealing that what awaits Sandra is not a steady career as a governess, but a nightmarish fate that has already befallen Victoria Vera. Cut to the other girl in the mad scientist's laboratory, heavily sedated and lashed to an operating table, leather straps crisscrossing her body and mask covering her face as the evil scientist cuts into her cranium. With one incision, he turns her into a living corpse, a walking dead girl who, instead of wreaking havoc, is doomed to be loaned out to satisfy the depraved fantasies of men like Lord Ferguson, who looks like he should be playing a bandit from the Sierra Morena. Now we know the orphanage's terrible secret—and Sandra does, too.

From here on, Sandra, in her white blouse, runs like a soul in torment, narrowly escaping all kinds of threats and torments, although by the end of the film she's bound and gagged as usual, back to the silent-movie routine: open eyes, shrieking mouth, body writhing in just the right way to make her breasts pop out of that white blouse. It's a ridiculous movie. Even Camus would say it's too absurd. We don't have to spend more time on it, but I just want you to know it ends with a cruel anagnorisis: Sandra learns that the man of her dreams, the good Dr. Kruger, is in fact the wicked, deformed scientist. You should really just watch *Dr. Jekyll and Mr. Hyde.*

"You could tell Sandra had never done theater," a famous actress who starred in Sandra's last movie, *Ángel negro,* told me. "She wasn't educated in that way."

Sandra was self-conscious on that front. In one interview, she said, "Now that I'm very close to having a real career, there are people out to get me. Saying I'm vain, or an exhibitionist, or only getting cast for my looks. None of that's true, but I can see why someone would get that idea from the movies I'm in. I've just had to be a good girl, a trained seal. You know how the industry is."

The interviewer asks if she feels that she's being objectified. Sandra replies, "I wouldn't say that. I mean, not more than happens to any woman. And when it happens, I always learn something from the experience. You know, I've learned a lot just being on set. I take classes in my free time—speech, movement, ballet—but my serious education happens when I get a script. I study my part, see how close I can get to the character, how completely I can understand her. Directors don't always want you to identify with your character, but I do. And when I'm rehearsing, I always tape myself so I can listen and correct my performance. I'd rather learn alone than get a coach, since in the end, the only person I'll always have by my side is myself. I'm especially proud of *Beatriz,*" she adds, "the movie I made with Gonzalo Suárez. I can't say whether the whole thing came out well or not, but I'm proud of how I handled my role."

The poster for *Beatriz* is a still of Sandra, her loose hair spilling over her shoulders. She wears a white blouse. She's wincing, eyes closed, as if the camera has caught her shrinking away from something—or, maybe, it's intruded on another sort of scene. Both of her shoulders and one of her breasts are exposed, though her right forearm chastely covers the latter: the censors would never have allowed it to show. She's tugging on her left sleeve with her right hand, though you can't tell whether the blouse is going on or off. It's an ambiguous, erotic image, standard for Spanish cinema at the time.

Beatriz is based on a handful of Valle-Inclán stories. Sandra's character is named Leonor again, but this time she's the daughter of a Galician countess played by Carmen Sevilla who lives in a remote but stately manor house. We don't need to waste time on the plot. Sandra has been cursed, or maybe possessed, and starts the movie hallucinating in bed, shivering and shrieking and convulsing until her breasts pop out of her white blouse. Eventually some bandits tie her up and hold her at knifepoint; a malevolent monk chases her through the woods at night; she has to kiss him, then begs for mercy, huddles in a ball of panic, the shot tightening around her eyes, which are full of hopelessness, terror, innocence, desire, temptation—the same role she always played.

It breaks my heart to envision her rehearsing in her room, wailing, "No, don't!" and "I'm begging you, please, please let me live!" and "Oh!" and "Ah!" and "Ayyy!" into her tape recorder. All that panting, all those muffled shouts and anxious gasps and sobs and unstoppable weeping, and never once, "O, what a noble mind is here o'erthrown! The courtier's, soldier's, scholar's, eye, tongue, sword, th' expectancy and rose of the fair state, the glass of fashion and the mould of form, th' observ'd of all observers, quite, quite down! And I, of ladies most deject and wretched, that suck'd the honey of his music vows," or, "When you durst do it, then you were a man; and, to be more than what you were, you would be so much more the man. Nor time nor place did then adhere, and yet you would make both. They have made themselves, and that their fitness now does unmake you. I have given suck, and know how tender 'tis to love the babe that milks me. I would, while it was smiling in my face, have plucked my nipple from his boneless gums and dashed the brains out, had I so sworn as you have done to this." No, Sandra Mozarowsky was never Ophelia, or Lady Macbeth, or Hedda Gabler.

"One must imagine Sisyphus happy," Camus concludes at the end of "The Myth of Sisyphus," having compared the absurd man—the man who knows, who's conscious of his mortality and of the futility of pursuing transcendence—to the Homeric hero condemned by the gods to eternally roll a boulder up a mountain. When Sisyphus is inches from the summit, the rock breaks free and tumbles down the slope, and he has to start again. Century after century, Sisyphus ascends the mountain, bearing the weight of the rock, which will roll to the bottom when he's about to achieve his goal, and down he goes, up, down, up, down—and Camus wants us to imagine him happy! He writes, "The struggle itself toward the heights is enough to fill a man's heart" (he doesn't speak of women's hearts). "It happens as well that the feeling of the absurd springs from happiness. 'I conclude that all is well,' says Oedipus, and that remark is sacred."

One must imagine Sandra happy, happy during the long nights and chilly mornings on set, happy in her coat, or maybe a bulky sweater, drinking coffee and chatting with the cast and crew while she waits for her call, getting ready to shed her coat and kick her shoes off the moment she hears "Action," to tremble barefoot in her white blouse with its elbow-length sleeves, its neckline that comes up to her collarbone, though in this scene or the next, by order of the script, it'll get undone to reveal a shoulder and breast, or else shredded, or spattered with blood, or crumpled on her exposed belly while some man's ass moves rhythmically between her open legs.

I've seen Sandra wearing that demure white blouse in *El mariscal del infierno*, in *La noche de las gaviotas*, in *El colegio de la muerte*, in *Beatriz*, in *Pecado mortal*, in *Special Train for Hitler*, in *Ángel negro*. I want it to have a meaning. Surely that virginal blouse isn't just a coincidence. It's a symbol, a signal, a sign pointing to—what? A bunch of male directors (she never worked with a woman) seeing her in a white blouse, liking the view, and repeating it? Could be. I'm pretty sure I got Camus's point about absurdity, so I'm not going to come up with a whole myth of the shirt. I'm not even going to keep asking why she played the same two roles—the damsel in distress and her reverse, the prostitute—so many times. Could a young actress in Spain aspire to anything else at the time?

At seventeen, Sandra complained to the press, "I'm sick of saying, 'Yes, this one is *destape*,' or 'No, it isn't *destape*.' Just flip a coin. Really playing a character is about a lot more than whether you have to take your shirt off. Sometimes you do, sometimes you don't." But by the time she got done shooting in Mexico, she'd changed her tune. She told *¡Hola!* she was "saying goodbye to movies" for a while, that she was "sick of always playing the same part, sick of script after script where I have to take my shirt off. I'm moving to London to study English and drama, then coming back to Spain for my baccalaureate, and *then* I'll act again. I love it more than anything else in the world, but I'm quitting until I have the qualifications that get you treated as more than an object."

One night Sandra appears on television. She's in her bedroom pouting and whining, bursting out of a white dress with heavy, pseudo-medieval silver embroidery. The comic actor Alfredo Landa appears in the doorway, wearing a white tunic over brown breeches and carrying some sort of instrument made of a ram's horn. Concerned, he asks, "What's wrong?"

"Oh, it's so awful," she says, weeping. "I'm so scared. My lock rusted, and I can't turn the key."

"What lock?"

"On my chastity belt! I put it on and now I can't get it off," Sandra says, raising her skirts to show a gilded chastity belt with a giant padlock. "Everyone's going to laugh at me. I'm going to have to call a locksmith. I'm so embarrassed. I wish I could just die."

But Alfredo Landa has an idea. He asks if she has a hairpin. She demurs, then admits she does. She sits on her canopy bed, takes a pin from her hair, and hands it to Alfredo Landa, who puts the tip in the lock and gets to work. Before long, Sandra's expression has changed. She's laughing with pleasure and delight, then falling on the bed, Alfredo Landa on top of her.

This work of cinema is called *Cuando el cuerno suena*, and it unites me and Sandra in eternity, or in my small, cluttered living room with its heaps of books and drafts and newspapers. I rent my apartment, so while it's my right to be here, I'm still a precarious resident—of my home and of time, unlike Sandra, who's returned from the dead on my screen. Camus was wrong to say actors' glory is ephemeral and fleeting. He wasn't thinking about movies or television, where even something as silly as *Cuando el cuerno suena* can live for all time. You could say it's not Sandra who's joined me, just her appearance, but Camus says the actor is his appearance, so here she is.

I'd rather be in Sandra's room, with its bulletin board covered with flags, photos, and souvenirs from her travels (she's been all over, thanks to her diplomat dad), its giant poster of Joan Crawford. A small guitar and a balalaika hang on a wall, and a Spanish guitar rests on a nearby stool. (I'm not inventing this; I saw her bedroom in the May 1975 issue of *ABC, Blanco y Negro*.) I imagine her in bell-bottoms and a loose white peasant blouse with short, embroidered sleeves. I'm thirteen but look eleven. I'm with my sister Blanca, who's fifteen but looks eighteen, a source of envy and admiration for me. She's Sandra's friend. I'm just tagging along. I'm shy and solitary, and sometimes Blanca feels sorry for me and lets me trail in her wake. Of course, I'm even shyer in Sandra's presence. She's an actress! You can see her in theaters! (Well, I can't see her, since *destape* is all rated R. My sister can't either, which is comforting.) Besides, Sandra's so pretty, and she has that hair. Blanca has great hair, too. Not me. My mother, who wears her hair short, made me get a pixie cut. Along with my thinness and total lack of curves, my hair means I regularly get mistaken for a boy, which causes me no end of anguish.

Sandra is rehearsing the lock scene for us. She pouts, exaggerates, rolls her eyes as she recites her dialogue. My sister cracks up when Sandra gets to the rusted-on chastity belt, and so I laugh too, a couple seconds late, not getting the joke in the slightest. After a while, with what strikes me as consummate grace, Sandra takes the guitar off the wall and launches into a Cecilia song: "Era feliz en su matrimonio, / Aunque su marido era el mismo demonio. / Tenía el hombre un poco de mal genio / Y ella se quejaba de que nunca fue tierno." My sister and I fake-sing along, opening our mouths and lip-synching without a sound. We're tone-deaf, and, each in our own ways, we try to hide it.

When the song ends, we both clap. Sandra reaches for her pack of cigarettes, puts one in her mouth, and offers them to Blanca. I get nothing. Maybe if I looked fifteen rather than eleven it would be different, or if I weren't so flat.

I ask my sister to share her cigarette with me—I have to do something; it's too humiliating to chew sunflower seeds as if we were in school—and she gives me a suspicious look, but hands over the cigarette, ordering me to only take one drag and not suck on it. I inhale two or three times, furtively, once she's not looking, then give it back, too nauseous to care that she and Sandra are now whispering to each other, telling secrets, laughing mysteriously, though of course I can guess what they're talking about: men, boys, boyfriends.

"Who was that boy at the bar last night?" my mom asked. I had no answer prepared. I'd thought she was too trashed to notice (not that I was any less drunk than she was; it was New Year's, and we had all celebrated unreservedly).

"Come on," she insisted. "I saw you with him. You were sitting between his legs on the stairs, and he was cuddling you and kissing your neck. I saw it all. So tell me, who was he?"

He was F., and he was my first love. My first *real* love, anyway. I was fifteen; he was twenty-two, an architect—well, an architecture student—like the heroes of my corner-store romances. I met him in Formigal over Christmas, and although our relationship didn't last long, it made a deep impression on me. I was in love! It was like the movies, like a book, like my very own daydreams, but deeper and better. Falling in love the first time is unique. Never again are you so happy, so surprised, so innocent. On the second round, you're wary from the start, aware that whatever you're beginning might end, probably *will* end, and therefore should be treated with caution. What you say or don't say, what you permit or tolerate or demand, is dictated by the lessons you've learned, the humiliations you've suffered, the calculated desire to avoid getting hurt or hurting someone else. Gone is your spontaneity, your blind confidence. Starting the second time around, love means pretense, reservations, machinations. Maybe that's why our first loves linger, shining eternally in our imaginations, even the ones that, like mine, lasted less than a month in reality.

What do I remember?

Sitting outside a club in his ultramarine Seat 127, a gin and tonic in my hand, flipping a coin to see who had to kiss who. I lost. I drank for courage, then leaned in and kissed him—I, who had never kissed anyone—on the lips. He could tell I had no idea what I was doing, and, to my great relief, assumed control from then on. I was ignorant, but I wanted to learn, and he was happy to be my teacher.

Skiing together, then holing up in his bedroom in the apartment he shared with his sisters, drinking more gin and listening to King Crimson and Leonard Cohen, who I'd never heard before. Inevitably, we wound up on top of each other in his bed, as was my goal. Still, I didn't put out. In the early seventies, a girl my age couldn't have sex and still call herself decent—or not in my mind, anyway. I was bound by the unspoken yet ironclad code of conduct that regulated precisely what was and was not permitted: anything above the waist was a go, but if a hand ventured downward, a nice girl had to learn how to say no, not that, not there. You said it regretfully, apologetically, without much conviction, but you said it. Your reputation was on the line. Men would lose respect for you if you didn't put the brakes on them. If you slept with a guy, he'd decide you were a slut and, after taking maximum advantage, ditch you. Besides, it was common knowledge that no one would date you if you weren't a virgin. I labored under the delusion that my friends, my sister, my sister's friends, my mother, and even my aunts were studying my behavior closely, scowling at my daring with F., waiting to see if I would commit even the smallest violation of the rules. And on top of all that, I didn't want him to get the impression that I was either loose or uptight. It required very complex diplomacy.

But F. couldn't have been more of a gentleman. He accepted my limits, resigning himself to essentially chaste cuddling without ever pushing or attempting to "take advantage." He charmed me, and, more surprisingly, he was *interested* in me. He listened; he paid attention, which I wasn't used to; he taught me all sorts of things. When I look back, I can't understand my appeal. Why was he hanging out with a naïve teenager? Presumably he started asking himself the same question pretty quickly, since it took him less than a month to change his mind.

After Día de los Reyes, winter break ended, and we had to part. I went home to Barcelona, and he returned to architecture school in Madrid. He called me from his dorm any time he got a chance, or so he said. For me, those calls were a lifeline, not that I got many. My mother had a habit, which she maintained until the day she died, of talking on the phone after dinner. It was her conversation hour. She'd park herself at the telephone table in our study with a glass of red wine, her cigarettes and ashtray, and her address book, and methodically call friends and family from 10:00 to 11:30 P.M. She never took breaks, and, therefore, F. never got through. What did she care? What did it matter to her if he had something major to tell me? She was busy giving a pep talk ("I'm telling you," she'd say, "you've got to leave him. He's gone too far. You don't have to put up with it a second longer. Call a lawyer tomorrow and get yourself separated from that bastard." A week later, she'd call the same friend and scold her for not taking her advice—my mother, who had more than enough reasons to leave my father and never did). All I could do was go into the study every so often and glare my hatred at her, or wring my hands to convey the gravity of the situation: I was missing a vital conversation with the love of my life so she could talk on the phone.

F. lived in Madrid; he had a car; he was an adult, and I was a high-school girl. In my mind, Madrid was swarming with temptations, meaning women and sexually liberated college students, and so when he mentioned he was going back to Formigal one weekend, I said I'd go, too. We reunited in Lérida, where I'd traveled by bus, and headed onward in his Seat 127, but a snowstorm shut the highways down. We had a sexless night in Sabiñánigo and arrived at the resort on Saturday morning. F. headed to his apartment, I to my parents'. I wasn't planning to be good the whole trip, though: I was turning sixteen on January 26th, and sixteen, I had decided, was an entirely permissible age to lose one's virginity. I thought F. might dump me if I made him wait longer, and I was out of patience, too. I was legitimately attracted to F., and I was massively curious about sex. But there was no moment during our trip for me to communicate any of my plans, which I had imagined announcing while in his arms, not after he put chains on the tires or got gas. My news called for tact, delicacy, a correct atmosphere, and so I never delivered it. I was too scared, and besides, he seemed remote and uncaring, which, I was sure, was the fault of my haircut. I'd gone to my mom's hairdresser, who, on her instructions, had cropped my hair shorter than ever. I looked even more like a boy than usual. No wonder F.'s enthusiasm had decayed.

After our return to Formigal, he dumped me, and oh, how I suffered! I'd had no idea a person could be in such profound, relentless pain. It was cruel that I had to sit in school, surrounded by my pimply peers, when an abandoned woman like myself couldn't possibly care about deciphering logarithms. I had a broken heart (which, I thought, *made* me a woman: age was irrelevant in the face of my misery, which was simply too great for a girl).

For years I dreamed of F., scouting for his license plate, which I knew by heart, in Barcelona, Menorca, even England, sure that if I let my guard down he would appear on a street I never could have expected: his car, then him, dressed in blue as usual. All the blood would drain from his face when he saw me. He wouldn't say a word. Our eyes would meet, and then he'd wrap his arms around me, kiss my face and neck, and recite the romance-novel lines I longed to hear: "Clara, I can't live without you. You're the love of my life."

Reality rarely hands out such rewards, though my imagination was generous with them. As it happened, I saw him that spring at the bar where we'd met. He had a new girlfriend, an eighteen-year-old with a long blond ponytail, a significant upgrade from me. I assume he saw me, but he didn't wave, let alone hurry to my side and, shaking, confess his undying love. For years, though, I told myself that he would.

I ran into him in Zaragoza decades later. We did some reminiscing, of course, and when our young romance came up, he said he'd freaked out when it hit him that I'd run away to join him in Formigal. And then, only then, the memory returned. I hadn't run away, but I'd lied to my parents, telling them our family friends' daughter, with whom I was close, had invited me to go skiing, and that my mother had guessed the truth only after I got on the bus. She worried, of course, since in that pre-cellphone era it was impossible to get ahold of me; for all she knew, I could have disappeared completely, and as a result, when F. and I arrived at the resort—this is the bit I repressed—the mountain director was waiting. He told me my mother was in a panic and was about to tell the Guardia Civil to start searching for me. I can imagine how startled and scared F. must have been. My little adventure could have landed him in a police interrogation room, where, as an adult man traveling with a minor who'd left home without telling her parents, his situation would have been very bad indeed. He was smart to turn the heat down, to end his relationship with me. Pavese says nothing is more dangerous than first love, and I was certainly dangerous for F.: a silly, scatterbrained girl who would have gone to any length to hold onto him, though I wouldn't have stretched myself out on a railroad track to be crushed. I wasn't that extreme. I was in love but not insane, or in love but not that much.

"I'm sure now that I've never fallen in love," said Sandra Mozarowsky. "If I had, I wouldn't have let the relationship end, no matter what. I thought I was in love a couple times, but no: it's all still a mystery to me." I easily could have gotten that statement from one of my dime-store romances, but no, it came from the September 1977 issue of *Pronto*, the one whose cover announced, "Sandra Mozarowsky Has Died." I doubt its veracity, as well as that of the claim Sandra supposedly made to *¡Hola!* that she "appreciates sincerity, athleticism, a poetic nature, and good looks more than anything else in a man," or the shocking admission to *Primera Plana* (Issue 30, Sept. 22nd to 28th, 1977) that she was a virgin, which we've already discussed. I can't see Sandra choosing to tell such a jealously guarded secret on the record. I feel equally skeptical about her profession of Catholic faith ("Of course I trust in God, the Father. I'm a Catholic. I know there's a heaven, and I wonder about hell. Could more than one hell be real?" she asks the *Primera Plana* reporter), given that she had an Orthodox funeral. My guess is that the piece is made up, even though the interviewer, José María Monís, tried to prove its veracity by including a photo of himself with Sandra on a three-seater sofa, plenty of room for the Holy Ghost between them, a cigarette in Sandra's right hand and a dog curled up on her lap.

Not long after the *Primera Plana* interview came out, *¡Hola!* released an "Emotional Goodbye to Sandra Mozarowsky" by someone named Santy Arriazu, who wrote, "We who knew her will never forget her green eyes, her smile, her warmth, her way of waving off a drink or a cigarette if you offered (she never touched alcohol or tobacco)." But Sandra smoked.

When my mother got drunk with her friends, she liked to

sing rancheras. Her favorite was "El rey," the Vicente Fernández version. She'd belt, "Con dinero y sin dinero, hago siempre lo que quiero, y mi palabra es la ley, no tengo trono ni reina, ni nadie que me comprenda, ¡pero sigo siendo el rey!" We sang it in her memory, just as off-key as she had (she wasn't ashamed of her tone-deafness), on the one-year anniversary of her death.

My mother was a monarchist ("In this house," she'd say, "we believe in the monarchy"), or she was for most of her life, just as she was a Catholic; at eighteen she considered the convent, but her life led her another way, and not long before dying she announced that she was an atheist. I suspect her other belief had weakened significantly by then, too, if it wasn't completely gone.

Her father, my grandfather Florentino, had wanted to die for his king, Alfonso XIII. His own father had fought the US in Cuba, and when our civil war began, my grandfather got himself out of Republican Barcelona and into Nationalist territory, where he joined the battalion of legionnaires that transformed into Franco's terrifying, brutal personal guard, in which he rose first to lieutenant, then, through his daring, captain. At the end of the war, he was among the vanguard in Barcelona (among its liberators, he would have said), returning to his family unscathed, triumphant, and obese (my dad, his son-in-law, always wondered how it was that during the war, when Spain was starving, my grandfather put on weight). In the meantime, his brother Pepe had joined an unsuccessful conspiracy to assassinate President Azaña, the last president of the Republic, then died in combat; another of his brothers, Eugenio Vegas Latapié, lived on, his monarchism burning so brightly it made the king himself look like a weak little republican.

Uncle Eugenio was the pride of my maternal family, the Vegases. He honored us with one visit when I was little, accompanied by his countess wife, who was the highly cultivated Madrid type you'd expect. My uncle, in my memory, is a delicate, ascetic being, very thin and pale, with my grandfather's high forehead and bony features. He and his wife, both of whom had beautiful manners, spoke and moved slowly and carefully, and I remember struggling to reconcile the fragile, fussy man before me with the firebrand my mother had described: a lawyer at eighteen, employed by the Council of State at twenty, personal advisor to the king five years after that. When the Republic was proclaimed on April 14th, 1931, Uncle Eugenio was one of the select committee of courtiers privileged to call on Queen Victoria Eugenia in Galapagar, where she went before leaving Spain (her husband Alfonso went on the run the second he lost his throne, not waiting for his wife and children), and once the royal family was safe and comfortable in France, Uncle Eugenio began working at a bank and conspiring to bring them back. He got fired and then imprisoned, but he wasn't deterred. Along with patriots like Ramiro de Maeztu and the Marquis of Quintanar, he was the wind beneath the (right) wings of the monarchist group and magazine Acción Española. After the general José Sanjurjo's failed coup in 1932, Uncle Eugenio got out of Spain for a while, but soon enough he was home and plotting once more. After the 1936 uprising, he tried hard to get the Prince of Asturias, the heir to the throne, into the Army, but his efforts were foiled by Mola, a general who, from then on, Uncle Eugenio feared was insufficiently monarchist (a failing of which he suspected all the anti-Republican generals, in fact). Eugenio joined the military three times himself, once under an assumed name in a company of legionnaires led by Captain-General Yagüe, who caught and expelled him immediately. It's touching, really, how badly Eugenio wanted to serve in a military whose commanders loathed him (and rightly so: he carried a last will and testament that said, "I die not for Franco, but for my king and queen").

Both he and his monarchs made it through the war, and he visited them in Rome, where they'd gone after France. He was badly disappointed in Franco, who won the war but, rather than restoring Bourbon rule, named himself king, though he used the strange honorific Generalissimo. In Rome, Uncle Eugenio persuaded Alfonso to give the crown to his son Juan. After Alfonso died, Eugenio accompanied the family to Lausanne, then Estoril. He served as political secretary to don Juan, the exiled (or should we say nonexistent) king, then became Prince Juan Carlos's tutor, which required him to move to Freiburg. Eugenio only separated from the royals when Franco decided that Juan Carlos should be educated in Spain, and he did so unwillingly, saying in his goodbye to the prince, "Should anyone dare suggest that I have abandoned His Majesty, understand that nothing could be further from the truth. Others prefer that I not continue at his side and I must therefore resign, but may God bless the prince and may he pray for me when he remembers, as a last kindness to his faithful servant, who loves him with his whole heart." He then returned to Spain and served in the government once more. Per his wishes, his tomb reads, *He lived and died true to his ideals* (or, as Camus put it, "what is called a reason for living is also an excellent reason for dying").

On the occasion of my parents' wedding, Uncle Eugenio gifted them a black-and-white portrait of Juan de Borbón in an imposing military uniform, and his wife, María de las Mercedes, in a gown and significant jewelry, posing beneath the royal seal. At the bottom of the photograph are the monarch's signatures and the handwritten dedication, *To María José and Luis Usón*, along with the year, 1958. My mother was proud of that gift for as long as she was a monarchist, and I never understood her enthusiasm; china, flatware, a record player, a radio, a tea or coffee set, those are gifts you appreciate, but a photo of two strangers—?

Uncle Eugenio wasn't the only member of my family who enjoyed a certain intimacy with Juan Carlos. I did too, if only briefly, on the street. He was coming out of a jewelry store in a posh part of Barcelona, flanked by two men dressed like he was in navy pants and white golf shirts whose collars were trimmed in the colors of the Spanish flag. I can't give you the royal version of events, but in mine, he was walking quickly, ignoring his surroundings, and slammed right into me. After the collision, neither of us apologized: we were both flustered, and it happened so fast. His Majesty got straight into an idling car, its door held open by a beefy young man in a suit (or, rather, in plainclothes, unless he was a bodyguard rather than a cop). I'd thought he seemed vaguely familiar, but only then did it hit me that I'd been knocked over not by a friend of my dad's or one of my colleagues' clients, but by Juan Carlos I of Spain.

Years ago, two of my young nephews were wrestling, and Adrián, the older one, not just beat his brother Tomás but pinned him on the ground and sat on top of him, holding his arms down so his brother couldn't move. I remember Tomás glowering upward, rageful and powerless, and spitting, "Who do you think you are, the king of Spain?"

CHAPTER 2

WAS SANDRA SLEEPING with the king?

Imagine the responsibility of playing the royal lover. In Spain, the king is the earthly incarnation of the state, the Fatherland, the flag, the nation itself, with all its constituent parts: he's the Army and the government, the Ministry of the Regions, of Foreign Affairs, of Justice and Relations with the Courts. He's a man, sure, with the usual muscles and bones, but mainly he's a symbol, a walking institution, damn near a demigod. Climbing under the sheets with him would be like wrapping yourself up in all those abstractions. A little inhibiting, no?

I want to get in Sandra's skin. I'm imagining myself naked in bed, awaiting the monarch, who I call—His Majesty? Sir? Juan Carlos? My liege? See, I can't even decide where to start. My anxiety consumes me. I'm sure when he does join me he'll recoil, then call out, "Who let this girl in here? Get her out!," since even in my late teens I was a board, no tits or ass or waist to grab. Sandra, in contrast, was an actress, who, by seventeen, was an old hand at sex scenes. She'd rolled in proverbial and sometimes literal hay with peasants, clergymen, gentlemen, family men, thieves, Nazis, Alfredo Landa . . . She could fake orgasms, ecstasy, passion, delight, repulsion, terror, you name it—an aptitude that I assume was useful offscreen as well as on.

Our early encounters with a new partner often involve some pretending, since it isn't easy to seem unrepressed and comfortable while naked in front of a stranger, no matter how relaxed and spontaneous and abandoned we try to seem; really, we're trying hard to remember our manners, to obey the norms that quietly govern even the steamiest moments. Our arms and legs can tangle and untangle, our torsos grind together, our eyes close in surrender or abandon, but in our heads, we're busily mapping the mysterious new body in our space—what are its limits, its quirks, why does it smell and feel and taste like that, and what's going on with its tongue?—all while acting as if nothing novel or unknown were going on. Only later, when the body in question is no longer new and our ardor has cooled or settled, do we quit faking, ditch our manners, and dare to express our true needs, like, "You're hurting me. Move your arm."

So let's imagine Sandra months into her affair, long after she's gotten over the king's kingliness, when she dares to say, "You're hurting me. Move your arm."

I can't be Sandra in this scenario. Let's see if I can be the king.

I am my own ideal, the cause I live and would die to serve, a commitment to which I was born and in which I am not alone but joined by legions of men, young soldiers, the soldiers in my military, all of whom are ready and waiting—I hope—to give their lives for me. I hold my head high as my armies parade before me, troops shouting in unison, "Viva el Rey!" My medals gleam on the breast of my dress uniform, which is as sober as my face. I never allow myself a smile or a blush, no excitement or confused murmurs of thanks; no, I look fearlessly, martially forward, and after the parade, the captains-general in their starched jackets come greet me, as do the rest of the generals, the ministers, the archbishops and cardinals and the president and regional dignitaries and the chiefs of the opposition parties and many, many (too many, if I may speak frankly) other figures of authority, all of whom offer their hellos and good wishes and linger until I grace them with my recognition, as well as a smile or comment or moment of affection (really, they appreciate anything at all) about which they can boast later on. I call them all "tú," including the ones twice my age, which is a small pleasure of my royal status. None of them are sure how to address me: am I Sir? Your Majesty? Should they use the royal "we" ("Sir, would we like a snack?") or the singular? But I'm a polite guy, and I simply put a friendly hand on my subject's shoulder and say, "Great idea. Let's go eat," as if we were alone, or as if I were one more member of the assembled crowd, not the principal dancer of a highly rehearsed ballet that begins only when I decide it does.

Once I give the sign, everyone processes behind me to the dining room, then waits respectfully behind their chairs until I take my seat. My table accommodates over a hundred of my subjects; you could never get it into any home but a palace like mine. All hundred diners eat at my pace, no matter how quickly I snack or how slowly I linger over my meal. Various subjects chat, or give speeches, or make toasts, and of course they applaud tremendously when I speak. Nobody rises until I do. Once I'm full, I stand, and after a reverent instant, my subjects shoot up in such unison you can hear the scrape of their chairs on the carpet—and then I sit! Down my subjects go, and once everyone is settled, I get up, sit down, get up, sit down, up, down, up, down, my companions imitating me every time. What a fun game!

I can't be king. I'm not taking it seriously.

And if a king is going to succeed, he has to be dead serious. He has to swallow his own hook, suspend his disbelief like Coleridge says you must in order to read poetry. A king has to convince himself of his legitimacy, his right to inherit a country, a task that can't be easy after the English, French, and Russian Revolutions undid his family's claim to divinity. Before, European royals could take refuge in the claim that their rule, and every one of their whims, was the Lord's will, but now the people have ideas about sovereignty, and monarchies have transformed into lay churches with popes, cardinals, and cathedrals, but no sign of God—and the kings and queens know this, but still persevere. In a way, their commitment is admirable, though it's not like they have a choice. A crown prince who never assumes a throne is no one. As heir, the meaning of his life is succession. Once he's sovereign, he's achieved his purpose. He's joined history. But what if it never happens? Poor failed prince! Poor outcast! Poor little throneless king!

Chekhov's "The Lady with the Dog," a short story about adultery, is much less tragic than *Anna Karenina* or *Madame Bovary*. Its lovers, Anna Sergeevna and Dmitri Gurov, carry out a forlornly docile, well-mannered affair. Near the end, Chekhov writes that Gurov "had two lives: an apparent one, seen and known by all who needed it, filled with conventional truth and conventional deceit, which perfectly resembled the lives of his acquaintances and friends, and another that went on in secret. And by some strange coincidence, perhaps an accidental one, everything that he found important, interesting, necessary, in which he was sincere and did not deceive himself, which constituted the core of his life, occurred in secret from others, while everything that made up his lie, his shell, in which he hid in order to conceal the truth—for instance, his work at the bank, his arguments at the club, his 'inferior race,' his attending official celebrations with his wife—all this was in full view. And he judged others by himself, did not believe what he saw, and always supposed that every man led his own real and very interesting life under the cover of secrecy, as under the cover of night."

I was a teenager when I first read "The Lady with the Dog," and that passage struck and saddened me. What truths could I hide in a sheath? My stealth cigarette-smoking? Other than that, my outer and inner selves were the same, and similarly boring. I couldn't wait for the moment when I had a real, interesting life to lead in darkness and secrecy.

Sandra Mozarowsky had a more public life than I ever could have: announcing her virginity in tabloids, telling the world that she enjoyed "singing and playing guitar with her friends," wanted to be an actress but not a star, loved to travel, had "lots of fantasies, but my only boyfriend is my job." Everyone knew that she bought her mom a present with her first acting paycheck, that her favorite actor was Robert Mitchum, that she wanted to "study law and become a diplomat" when she grew up. As for her private life, the one in the sheath of secrecy, the internet will tell you it involved a job at a strip club on Madrid's Calle Oriente. Supposedly the club belonged to Paco Martínez Soria, the actor who played some of Spanish cinema's greatest hicks—he starred in *La ciudad no es para mí*, *El turismo es un gran invento*, *Abuelo made in Spain*, and so on—a big pet of the Franco regime. Or perhaps Sandra worked in another club in Madrid, this one called La Poupée, where the waitresses, or "dolls," wore see-through uniforms to pass canapés through the crowd. According to *Nadiesocial's Blog*, "La Poupée was open Monday through Saturday, and the waitresses took home three thousand pesetas a night, a pretty good wage back then. All of them had a certain aura, a way of treating people, an ability to listen. A good number were studying law or medicine or architecture, paying for school by pouring drinks at Madrid's most select club. Every single one was discreet, serene, cultured, and so gorgeous you wanted to die."

It's not hard to imagine a half-naked Sandra smiling as she offers her tray of hors d'oeuvres (offers herself) to older men, creepy Francoist heavyweights who run their eyes over her body while eating their smoked salmon, assessing her, and then whisper a suggestion or day or number in her ear, mustaches wet and tongues laden with crumbs. Of course it's not hard: I've seen her play versions of this role, the new escort or the experienced whore, in nearly all her movies. In life, though, I doubt she would have bothered. Her family was well off, and she earned good money onscreen. She had an agent, Rosa García, who she mentions gratefully in interviews. Rosa got Sandra roles and accompanied her to the set of her last movie, *Ángel negro*, which shot in Colombia. One of Sandra's Spanish co-stars told me that each actor got a cabin for the months of filming, and that Sandra shared hers with Rosa, who watched out for her, protected her, fussed over her like a second mother. While everyone else was partying and going wild, Sandra and Rosa had their own little life. Sandra was a sweet young woman, a little shy or timid, very ambitious. She was on a strict diet, which her agent supervised, and she never got high and rarely drank. She really was a good girl.

Which was the real Sandra? A serious, careful artist on the rise, or a hot little cocktail waitress? A young innocent or a young whore? Could she have contained both?

Sandra Mozarowsky appears as Juan Carlos I's secret girlfriend on various blogs, vlogs, and websites, including Wikipedia (with more detail in English than Spanish), and in the English journalist Andrew Morton's *Ladies of Spain*, a study of the Spanish monarchy. Morton writes, "Supposed royal lovers included, among others, the Italian singer Raffaella Carrà and the very young actress Sandra Mozarowsky." Meanwhile, Rebeca Quintans, author of an unauthorized biography called *Juan Carlos I: La biografía sin silencios*, claims that "the monarch often had his staff bring him the girls he enjoyed watching on television. Sandra wasn't the only one: Sara Montiel, Raffaella Carrà, Nadiuska, and Bárbara Rey received similarly ignoble summons to the palace."

What a moment! Peak seventies, Franco dying, new reports coming from his doctors constantly, Juan Carlos getting ready to ascend the throne . . . On November 22nd, 1975, when he was crowned king, I was fourteen. What could I have thought? What could any Spaniard have thought of our sexy new sovereign? Jokes circulated quietly, suggesting he wasn't the sharpest tack in the drawer. No one thought he'd do much or last long;

right away, we called him Juan Carlos the Brief. Why get our hopes up for Franco's puppet? Year after year, we'd seen him in the Día de la Hispanidad military parades, trotting beside his master in matching olive uniforms heavy with medals, posing with the Caudillo as if they were father and son. We'd heard Juan Carlos praise Franco, defend the dictator's internationally reviled choice to execute five political prisoners, grieve at his deathbed, and swear after the Generalissimo passed to uphold his laws, to "obey them and have them obeyed." Again: why get our hopes up?

Oh, and everyone knew Juan Carlos had murdered his brother. It was never reported, and yet it was common knowledge that during Holy Week of 1956, when King Juan de Borbón and his family were living in exile at Villa Giralda in Estoril, Portugal, Juan Carlos and his little brother Alfonso were playing with a gun and the older boy accidentally shot the younger in the head, killing him. Official accounts said the fourteen-year-old prince shot himself, but the truth emerged and eventually made it into sanctioned royal biographies. Supposedly, don Juan, who always preferred his second son, demanded of Juan Carlos, "Swear to God it wasn't intentional."

Alfonso was buried hurriedly, without a police investigation or autopsy, and Juan Carlos, who was eighteen, got packed back off to the Spanish military school where he was already a cadet. Portugal's dictator, António de Oliveira Salazar, did his friend Franco a favor and made sure nobody looked any further into the event, even though don Juan's brother Jaime wrote a letter demanding a judicial investigation, arguing, "As the head of the house of Bourbon, it's my duty to seek justice; as a man, I can't accept that a person who has never learned to take responsibility might someday ascend to the Spanish throne." No one cared, though (and no one considered Prince Jaime head of the house of Bourbon). Not one Spaniard was surprised to see a prince evading accountability; we never for a second thought he would have to suffer consequences as if he were a commoner. In Spain, the legal system can't reach the powerful. I'm a lawyer, and I can tell you that an eighteen-year-old is an adult, and an adult—especially one with military training and a deep familiarity with guns—accidentally shooting and killing a child is a homicide. Second-degree, yes, or manslaughter, but it's homicide, which should mean a trial and a non-negligible prison term. Maybe that threat, or its conspicuous absence, helped Juan Carlos see his great and gleaming future: if Franco, who hated his father, hadn't planned to crown him king, he wouldn't have interceded. Cadet Juan Carlos de Borbón might easily have gone to jail, but as monarch-to-be, he was immune, untouchable, high in the celestial realm beyond right and wrong.

What else? We all knew Juan Carlos looked down on his dad.

Prince Juan Carlos was the son of an exiled king, a king with no country, an aspiring king who could only reclaim his crown if the tyrant who took it from him chose to give it back. A curse hung over the Bourbons: the Army controlled their access to the throne. Spain has no affection for its monarchs. We've kicked them out every chance we've gotten (see: 1931, when we started the Second Republic, though it was quickly squashed by Franco and his goons), and not once has there been public clamor to bring them back. Just as Fernando VII required the English army and the Cien Mil Hijos de San Luis to give him his crown back in 1823 (his widow, María Cristina, then got re-expelled from the country); just as his daughter Isabel II, dethroned by the army during the Glorious Revolution in 1968, cooled her heels in Paris until General Arsenio Martínez Campos rose up against the First Republic and put her son Alfonso XII on the throne; just as Alfonso XIII needed yet another soldier, Miguel Primo de Rivera, to prop him up (not that well: he wound up losing his seat and dying in Rome), Alfonso XIII's son, Juan de Borbón, sat in Portugal, wondering with a mix of impatience and resignation whether the general who'd taken Spain away from him would decide to give it back—and, if so, when. Would Franco get sick of ruling? Would he die in power? Of course he did the latter, having enjoyed every moment of his control.

We should note, in Juan Carlos's defense, that he was born in 1935, when the rock of the Bourbon dynasty had just tumbled to the bottom of the cliff. Hauling it up again seemed an enormous task, superhuman, too challenging even for Sisyphus. It's said that the ends justify the means, and Juan Carlos's end was recovering the Spanish throne for the Bourbons. As for his means, well, sometimes a royal has to get in the muck like the rest of us, has to praise a dictator (a usurper!) and plot against his own dad. In 1966, Prince Juan Carlos told *Time* solemnly, "I would never accept the crown in my father's lifetime." In 1969, Franco named Juan Carlos his successor as king. Juan Carlos said yes gladly, then asked don Juan for his blessing.

Instead of going along, his father said irritably, "What are you saving? A monarchy that dethroned me? A Francoist monarchy? You haven't saved us. You haven't restored our dynasty or gone through the order of succession. I don't bless you, I will never bless you, and I will never accept you as king of

Spain." As proof of his anger and disapproval, he retracted his son's title. Juan Carlos was no longer Prince of Asturias, which created an issue: how can a person be king *in pectore* when he isn't even a prince? Franco resolved the situation by inventing a new role, calling Juan Carlos the Prince of Spain—which means, according to strict monarchists, that Franco, a general without so much as a drop of blue blood, didn't bring back the House of Bourbon. It was highly irregular for him to give Juan Carlos a title, let alone name him king; in doing so, he created a new monarchy, one that descended from him, Francisco Franco, and that could just as easily have begun not with Juan Carlos but with Franco's chauffeur, or his barber, or his son if he'd had one. Nobody in Spain would have said a word.

For years, Juan Carlos suffered the humiliations of praising a tyrant, posing with him, yielding to his ego, and putting up with his endless vigilance, anything to ensure that Franco didn't change his mind about who got to ascend to the throne. He'd said Juan Carlos would succeed him, yes, but he could easily name someone else, maybe Juan Carlos's cousin Alfonso, who'd married Franco's granddaughter. So Juan Carlos played the yes-man, the faithful courtier, he, who was born to be king!, and his iron loyalty worked. In 1975, the Bourbons, in the person of Juan Carlos I, ascended the Spanish throne once more, by the grace of the soldier Francisco Franco. In that very moment, don Juan learned that the end does indeed justify the means: he renounced his dynastic rights in favor of his son, which, on the one hand, spared him the disgrace of becoming the inaugural Francoist monarch, but, on the other, meant he got the consolation of having sired a king.

And so Juan Carlos the Brief achieved his life's goal. He was on the dais, lodged on his throne, all by himself—for how long? A soldier had put him there; another one could always come knock him down. Juan Carlos had learned his dynasty's tragic tradition, and, traveling through Spain, he'd seen that he wasn't popular in the slightest. Nominally, he had the powers of an absolute monarch, but really, he was at the army's mercy. We were shocked, then, when he shook the generals' arms from around his shoulders, demonstrating an acuity we'd never thought he had, acquiring some legitimacy. A fratricidal king who betrays his father sounds like a Shakespeare tragedy, like *Macbeth* or *Richard the Third*, but if Juan Carlos came from a book it would be *The Leopard*, Giuseppe di Lampedusa's drama of the Risorgimento, and he'd be Falconeri, the hero's nephew, a handsome, ruined young prince who abandons his family to join Garibaldi, having seen the old order decaying and guessed that if he wants things to stay as they are, things will have to change.

An absolute monarchy installed by a dictator wasn't just inconceivable in Europe at the end of the twentieth century: it was *uncool*. After Franco died, the Americans, who had condoned and supported his regime, suggested that we should have a starter democracy, a system that would transform Spain into a nation that could join NATO someday. Our European neighbors—the Brits, the French, the Germans, the Italians—scorned our regressive new rule, which struck them as something that belonged in a former colony, not in Europe. As for us, the Spanish (the majority, anyway), how we dreamed of normality! If we had a regular, ordinary democracy, we could emerge from the peninsula on which we were sequestered, hidden by the Pyrenees and forgotten by God, and, after so much waiting, join Europe. Democracy, freedom of speech, amnesty, a statute of autonomy—we shouted for those things in the streets. At my progressive school, where we spent our eternal assemblies debating the human and divine or voting via raised hand or speechifying about our opinions, we never got sick of the magic words "freedom" and "democracy."

I was fourteen when I went to my first protest. My class had decided to show solidarity with the stevedores at the port, who were striking. Our teacher herded us there, careful to keep us safe and far away from any skirmishes with the cops, who we called the *grises* and of whom we were terrified, since they used real ammunition on demonstrators back then. Walking to the port, I asked my teacher what "stevedore" meant—never hurts to know who you're showing solidarity with—and wrote the answer in pen on my wrist. I maintained that habit for years: writing new words on my skin so I would remember to look them up in the dictionary when I had a chance.

Juan Carlos understood instantly that as an absolute monarch, he should live up to his nickname the Brief. He tapped Adolfo Suárez, a shadowy, unknown member of Franco's cabinet, to be president, and from there he launched a transformation of the Spanish crown. In November 1976, a referendum approved the Political Reform Law, which turned us into a parliamentary monarchy, gave amnesty to all political prisoners, and sanctioned their parties, including the Communist Party of Spain. Years later, a reporter named Victoria Prego asked Suárez in an interview whether the law also sanctioned the monarchy. "Of course," he said, "but I'm not saying how."

He *did* say how, though, once he thought his mic was cut.

You can hear his answer on YouTube. "Foreign leaders were always saying I should do a referendum on the monarchy," he said. "We got some polling, and Juan Carlos would've lost. So we just stuck the words 'king' and 'monarch' into the law, and presto! It had been put to a referendum already."

Our choices, in short, were a parliamentary monarchy or an absolute one. Ninety-four percent of Spain voted for the Political Reform Law, which got us on a path to the former. In October 1978, the constitution was approved. Suárez's clever maneuver ("we just stuck the words 'king' and 'monarch' in") made the monarchy seem natural, legitimate, even popular, and, in so doing, helped the new Bourbon dynasty get rid of its unpleasant Francoist sheen.

From then on, we had no more portraits of paunchy old Franco in government offices, gut stuffed in his uniform and crossed by a satin sash. Now we got a tall, handsome, fair-haired king in a jacket cut like a Hollywood actor's. During the dictatorship, the omnipresent image of the Generalissimo oppressed us, made us cowardly, reminded us of the despotism and surveillance under which we lived. In contrast, our new king wasn't so bad. He might've been a nice guy. He certainly wasn't a threat. As far as we could tell, he had his own concerns; he wasn't interested in what we were up to.

I doubt the king was interested in what *he* was up to: solemn masses, military parades, traditional dances, official receptions, audiences with foreign dignitaries and diplomats. A king's public life isn't enviable, as such. But his private life! His secret life! I, for one, envy that.

Surely, when Juan Carlos ascended to the throne, a chorus of friends warned him to abstain from affairs and adultery, from meddling and intriguing, from business—"A monarch's not a shopkeeper, Sir"—from dalliances and bastards and schemes of the sort that brought down María Cristina, Isabel II, and Alfonso XIII (Alfonso XII was spared not by good behavior, but untimely death), and presumably he promised to obey this good advice, but history, especially the royal kind, loves to repeat itself: his three great passions, women, business, and hunting, would lead him to abdicate in 2014, but in 1978, that was far away. He was our shiny young king, emerging unscathed from the past, making his debut on the throne.

In 1976, Sandra appeared in an episode of the historical drama *Curro Jiménez*. Was that when the king fell for her? What would a seventeen- or eighteen-year-old girl have discussed with a thirty-nine-year-old man who wasn't just twice her age, but was king? Did they talk about her ambitions, or her movies (in 1977, she made six: *Abortar en Londres, Special Train for Hitler, Hasta que el matrimonio nos separe, Pecado mortal, El espiritista,* and *Ángel negro*)? Or was he the one carrying the conversation, since she was shy, young, and inexperienced, and he was the ruler of Spain? Maybe she listened, entranced, green eyes wide with fascination (we've all seen that look) while he talked about his childhood, his adolescence, his relationship with Franco. Maybe he was too busy, or too married, to waste valuable time on chitchat. Maybe he talked about the weather, or her beauty, or the intricate negotiations he was carrying out to get the constitution done to all the political parties' satisfaction, which, if I were as ambitious a writer as Sandra was an actress, I'd be writing about now: no more Sandra, but the constitutional project that kept the king up at night.

I'd get to work on the most rigorous possible evocation of that great historic moment, the glorious transition, the complicated and (I assume) intense arguments between representatives of different parties: Herrero de Miñón, Pérez-Llorca, Peces-Barba, Solé Tura, Fraga Iribarne, Roca Junyent. I'd go through the constitution bit by bit, but this is a small story, a story about Sandra waiting and waiting and waiting for Juan Carlos, who's hours late, hasn't even called, and as the sun goes down some royal equerry takes pity on her and calls to say how sorry His Majesty is, but he's missing their date only because he's trapped in a meeting with Manuel Fraga Iribarñe, Gabriel Cisneros, and Jordi Solé Tura, or else with the American ambassador, or else with the apostolic nuncio, and that very meeting is going to decide Spain's destiny—which Sandra wants to believe, really she does, but the king has already stood her up once, and she torments herself about it. She suffers; she's suspicious; she has a sneaking feeling that if she's lost out to someone in a dress, it's not the reverend archbishop with his long skirt, but Nadiuska or Bárbara Rey, her acting friends, her rivals.

One must imagine Sandra in love with the king. He came straight from a fairytale, and she would have pined for him the way I did for the crown princes in my babysitter's tales. He was tall and handsome, kind and good-natured, and she would have gotten excited when she saw him on television in his dress uniform or his tailcoat, his perfectly tailored suits, surrounded by illustrious, elegant bald men or appearing in step with his long-suffering wife, Queen Sofía, who Sandra does not and will never consider a rival. Imagine Sandra hiding her emotions, blushing uncontrollably, gripped by a splendid triumph, an overwhelming pride that nearly cons her into shouting in public, "He's mine, the king of Spain is mine, he belongs to me!"

In "The Myth of Sisyphus," Camus looks at the legendary seducer Don Juan. According to Camus, "If it were sufficient to love, things would be too easy. The more one loves, the stronger the absurd grows. It is not through lack of love that Don Juan goes from woman to woman. It is ridiculous to represent him as a mystic in quest of total love. . . . If he leaves a woman it is not absolutely because he has ceased to desire her. A beautiful woman is always desirable. But he desires another, and no, this is not the same thing. . . . What Don Juan realizes in action is an ethic of quantity, whereas the saint, on the contrary, tends toward quality." Maybe Sandra dreamed of convincing Juan Carlos to choose quality, of becoming his only lover, the one who gave him "what no one else has ever given him." Of the women who tried to do so for Don Juan, Camus writes, "Each time they are utterly wrong and merely manage to make him feel the need of that repetition. 'At last,' exclaims one of them, 'I have given you love.' Can we be surprised that Don Juan laughs at this? 'At last? No,' he says, 'but once more.'"

CHAPTER 3

LUDWIG WITTGENSTEIN WROTE, "When one shows someone the king and says: 'This is the king,' this does not tell him the use of this piece—unless he already knows the rules of the game." I worry that Sandra never learned the rules. Wittgenstein devoted his life to deciphering them.

Born in Vienna in 1889, he was the son of a steel magnate, Karl Wittgenstein, the richest man in Austria and one of the richest in Europe. Ludwig was the youngest of nine; his family home was a palace. His mother, Leopoldine Maria Josefa Kalmus, Poldy for short (my mother, another María Josefa, went by Pepa), was a constitutionally nervous, weak woman, prone to anxiety attacks and intimidated by her cold, tyrannical husband. Music was her only source of comfort, and she passed her passion for it on to her children. Hans, the oldest, showed signs of prodigy at four and was compared to Mozart. Another son, Paul, was a brilliant pianist who, after losing his right arm in the First World War, gained international renown for his left-handed playing; it was for him that Ravel composed the celebrated Piano Concert for the Left Hand. Ludwig, meanwhile, invented and built a sewing machine when he was eleven years old.

Sandra was precocious too, in her way: she acted in *El otro árbol de Guernica* at ten. But I was much more precocious than she was. I got drunk for the first time when I was two. My parents used to have their friends over for dinner on Sundays, then go watch the bullfights, leaving me and my sister—this was before my brothers were born—with a sitter. One night, on returning from the plaza, they found a scene even more dramatic than the one they'd just left: a highly excited two-year-old me chasing my sister and the poor babysitter with a broom, slurring and stumbling like a drunk, which I was. Quickly my parents guessed what had happened. Rather than cleaning up, they had abandoned their friends' half-empty glasses of wine and gin and cognac on the coffee table, and I'd emptied them when the babysitter wasn't paying attention. My parents thought this was hilarious. In the morning, presumably, I had my first hangover, which didn't prevent me from repeating my mischief the next Sunday. My parents were less entertained that time, and from then on, my mother took the precaution of dumping everyone's glass out into the sink.

Such an episode would have been unimaginable in the Wittgenstein palace. Bullfights were not among Karl and Poldy's cultural interests. Karl Wittgenstein was a major art collector and generous patron who commissioned sculptures from Auguste Rodin and underwrote the painters of the Vienna Secession, an art movement promoted by Gustav Klimt, who did a portrait of Karl's daughter Gretl, but the true family obsession was music. Poldy was a pianist, and all nine children played instruments. In the palace, there were seven pianos and, on the ground floor, a grand Musiksaal in which the family held recitals featuring Brahms, Mahler, Schoenberg, Richard Strauss, and other luminaries. Although Ludwig was no Hans or Paul, he could whistle a whole symphonic movement without leaving out a note and was generally unimpressed by the great men who frequented the Musiksaal. In his opinion, "Music came to a full stop with Brahms." What would he have said about the concert nights at my parents' house, the ones when a music-loving friend got out the old guitar my mom kept in a closet and launched into "Cucurrucucú paloma" or "Amanecí en tus brazos" or "Cielito lindo" or "Clavelitos," accompanied by an eager chorus of drunks?

Ludwig would have been miserable in my house, and I in his. I'm too tone-deaf to have cared when my parents and their friends were off-key. My bad pitch would have made me the shame and laughingstock of the Wittgensteins. (My mother, like Karl, was an occasional patron of the arts, and once hired an out-of-work Argentinian who she'd met at a party to teach me and my sister guitar. A true artist, he devoted months to teaching us "Ojos verdes," but neither of us got as far as the chorus, and the sounds of our clumsy hands on the strings must have been torture to him. One afternoon, he confessed, wet-eyed, that he couldn't bear it any longer, and there went the second teacher I defeated with my giftlessness—another sign of my astonishing precocity.)

Yes, I would have been bored out of my mind listening to Brahms or Mahler in the Wittgenstein palace, and Ludwig would have been appalled to hear himself bellowing "Con dinero y sin dinero, hago siempre lo que quiero, y mi palabra es la ley" along with my family. A boy like him, raised by swarms of nannies and servants, taught by twenty-six private tutors, would never have known how to go buy his parents two bottles of wine at Antonio's bodega in Plaza Artós, which I could do by myself at age seven. On the other hand, if he had made it there and if the bodega owner had asked if he'd written to the Reyes Magos yet (shyly, excitedly, I said, "I did"), then jeered, "Aren't you too old to believe in them? You're getting those presents from your parents, not the Three Kings," he wouldn't have been too shocked and bereft to reply, like I was. He'd simply have said, "Whereof one cannot speak, thereof one must remain silent." (And in fairness, at that age I knew who my father was cheating on my mother with, and whereof one cannot speak, thereof one must remain silent.)

Wittgenstein's mother, Poldy, was a timid, melancholic introvert. Her children must have fought for her attention, tried to get her to shield them from their angry, demanding tyrant of a father. My mother, Pepa, wasn't shy in the slightest: the opposite, in fact. She made friends quickly, then remained loyal to them. She preferred their company to ours, and when we pissed her off, she'd say, "I'd be out having fun with my friends if it weren't for you!" She had a degree in philosophy (but wouldn't have graduated if it weren't for me: I cried so much in the night as a baby that she had no choice but to stay up and read), and yet the only profession she ever had was raising kids and keeping house for her husband. She made a couple halfhearted attempts at getting a job over the years, but my father never supported her. He'd made the division of labor clear from the start: she would handle the home and children and he would handle the money. In that time (that century), middle-class women didn't work. It was tacky. A woman only got a job if she was widowed or married to a man who couldn't support his family, and under no circumstances would my father have allowed her to give others the impression that he couldn't provide. In fact, he provided my mother two maids to help with the housework, and so her days of waiting for her children to return from school and father from work (if he was having dinner at home, that is) must have crawled. She must have gotten bored, my mother, and if she did, that explains many of the mysteries of my childhood.

Unlike Poldy, Pepa never neglected her children. She signed us up for every enrichment on offer: tennis class, English class, French, ballet, golf, sailing in summer. It was endless, and we were useless. Imagine if, instead of herding around a bunch of Usóns, she'd had the luck of parading the Wittgensteins from activity to activity. She'd have gotten to bask in applause and awards. But her kids were awful at tennis, mediocre at golf, too scared of water to sail. We were a little better at skiing, but that just meant my mother, to her great regret, had to spend her weekends driving hundreds of kilometers to the remote slopes where we competed and, inevitably, fell or got disqualified or at best came in seventh or ninth. But she never gave up. She never wore out. Her life's mission was herding us, hauling us, showing us, and she devoted herself to it, though not sweetly and sacrificially. She wasn't that good at lying to herself. In my memories, my mom was almost always in a bad mood. And I was afraid of her.

My mother was not an early riser. In the daytime, we children ate in the kitchen, and we didn't dare violate the sanctity of the living room until we got home at 6:00, when we were not only allowed but required to open its smoked-glass French doors. My mother was usually napping on the sofa, and, before entering, Pablo, Blanca, and I, the three oldest, negotiated unhappily over who had to open the door. No one wanted to wake her up, which made her mad. Without fail, she shouted at us, but we still had to bend and kiss her, inhale her cigarette- and liquor-rich breath.

She wasn't always in a bad mood. Sometimes she taught us world capitals, or did a puzzle with us, or served as the wardrobe department and audience for our theater productions. Sometimes she let us make fun of her, sometimes she recited Rubén Darío ("Margarita, how beautiful the sea"), sometimes it was a joy to be with her, but I was an expert at interpreting her signs—her tone, her tapping feet, her brightening eyes—and when I saw a storm coming I fled. I had no idea, could have had no idea, that her sudden changes of temper and eruptions of anger had nothing to do with us.

Brahms, a regular at the Wittgenstein palace, was surprised by its formality, the ceremony with which its inhabitants interacted, "as if they were at court," but those were the rules in the Wittgenstein family. All families have rules, and children learn to obey them, or to disobey by choice, long before understanding their logic. Even a small child can read in their dad's face or mom's gestures what can and cannot be said or done, and we Usóns were no exception. Consider the rule of the keys: if my father, on coming home, struggled and fought a long time with the doorknob, then we scurried straight to our bedrooms, not giving any guff or even waiting to be told to get out of adult territory ("Go to your rooms, kids, your dad's home"), just taking our games far from what was happening in the living room, which was our way of following the rules, even if my parents sometimes disobeyed them by getting in screaming fights at dawn, slamming doors and smashing glass in spectacular fashion, waking us up—that was part of a different game that also involved my mom bursting into Blanca's and my room crying, shakily approaching our beds, the miasma of chaos thickening in the room. I'd pull the sheets over my head and fake sleep, wishing for her to go away. I knew what was happening, but I didn't want to. I didn't want to be confronted by the evidence, since what was there for me to do with it?

My siblings and I used to play house, or, rather, Blanca and I made Pablo play with us, since we needed a male presence to give the game verisimilitude. Blanca or I took turns being the mother; whoever's turn it wasn't got to be the baby or grandmother or sitter. "Pablo," the mom would say, "time for the baby's bath," or, "Pablo, dinner's on the table."

"I'm in Madrid," our brother would reply. "I won't be back till tomorrow," and we'd get angry at him: that wasn't the right way to play! He was breaking the rules! Really, though, Pablo was playing his part to perfection. He was a father like ours, and Blanca's and my indignation was the mirror of our parents' discord.

Now let's have my parents play house. My mother would have said, "Luis, the water's ready, time to give Miguel his bath," (this is a complete fantasy: she never said that in real life) or, "Luis, it's so nice out, let's go for a walk" (also made up).

"I'm in Madrid," my dad would have replied. "I'll be back Friday." Or maybe, "My afternoon got tricky. I'm not going to be home for dinner." My mom would hang up the phone, sad and defeated, not saying aloud that he wasn't playing right; he was breaking the rules.

If the illustrious Ludwig had been there, he would have consoled her. He would have sat on a pouf in the living room, across from my mother on the—her—sofa, and said, "You shouldn't get mad at Luis. It's a question of the use of language, the function of words. 'Marriage' signifies one thing to you, another to him. You're playing different games while imagining you're playing the same one."

My mother would have sighed smoke out of her nose and mouth (she always had a cigarette on the go). "I don't know what to tell you, Ludwig. Want some whisky?"

He would have rejected the drink, horrified, and tried to steer her toward silence and discretion: whereof one cannot speak, thereof one must remain silent. My mother would have been the horrified one then. She loved to talk, and she would have wanted nothing more—since Luis wasn't coming home for dinner and they had plenty of time—than to tell that snooty Austrian how well things had started, how much fun she and her hot new husband had on their honeymoon in Pamplona and Sanfermines, neither one sober from the day they left to the day they returned. She'd thought that was how marriage would be; had thought it meant freedom, finally, no more obeying her father, doing whatever she liked; but instead she made the bitter discovery that she had merely traded one overlord for the next. Sure, her dad wasn't telling her what to do, but her husband was, and besides, what could she do with one two three four five children, like five iron balls chained to her ankles, never mind that she was a modern woman, a progressive woman, who had studied and who could smoke and drink as much as a man, if not more. Still she was condemned to spend the hours, the months, the years waiting for and on her husband and children.

"I hate this game, Ludwig," she might have said. "I want to play another one." It was impossible, though, and she knew it. In Franco's Spain, a married woman could only play house.

Now let's trade me to the Wittgensteins', where I'm the tenth child, Klara (it has a nice sound, Klara Wittgenstein), and my father, Karl, is furious, as always, but today's anger is special: none of my brothers—not Hans, not Rudi, not Kurt or Ludwig or Paul—wants to study engineering or follow him into business as he'd hoped. His sons have let him down. All five are squirrelly, neurotic, tortured, artistic souls without a speck of vitality or, even worse, virility. I try to comfort him. Unlike my sisters Gretl, Hermine, and Helena, I'm no shrinking violet. I'm not feminine or delicate. I can't paint or sew or play piano (or any other instrument, even the triangle). I'm going to fulfill his desires, make his dreams come true. I'm going to be an industrial engineer!

"Don't be absurd," thunders Karl.

My father Luis was similarly disappointed to realize that not one of his three sons planned to join him in the law. He wanted to hand his practice off to one of them. I studied law, but I didn't count; being a lawyer was what he did, which meant it was for men. He hoped I would switch to something, anything, that would assure me a quiet, undemanding government job, a lack of faith in my abilities that, I think, pushed me to decide I really would become a lawyer, even if my only true ambition in doing so was proving him wrong. (I practiced for fifteen years, and, once I thought I had demonstrated conclusively that I, a woman, could do my dad's job, I lost all interest, which probably validated his belief that women are inconsistent, flighty, and ill-equipped for the demands of the law.)

Hans, Rudi, and Kurt Wittgenstein did not see old age. For them, dying by suicide was the price they paid for violating the family rules, rejecting the paternal mandate. Hans, the oldest, the prodigy—his first word was "Oedipus"—vanished while canoeing on an American lake. His body was never found, and though people spoke of an "accident," his family eventually conceded publicly that he had taken his own life. He was homosexual and had already shown signs of suicidal ideation. When he died, in October 1902, he was twenty-four years old.

Two years later, also—perhaps as a homage—in October, Rudi Wittgenstein, whose father had forced him to study chemistry in Berlin but whose real interests were theater, photography, and music, walked into a café one night and ordered two glasses of milk. He bought the pianist a bottle of mineral water and requested the hit ballad "Verlassen, verlassen, verlassen bin ich." As its languid chords sounded, he dissolved an envelope of cyanide in his milk. He was twenty-four. He, too, was homosexual, and tormented by what he called his "perverted disposition." He was buried quietly in Vienna, and his father prohibited the uttering of Rudi's name in his presence.

Kurt Wittgenstein shot himself in the temple in a trench during World War I. His sisters were surprised. He was the happy one in the family.

Although Ludwig did not die by suicide, he started considering it at age ten. He always had the sense that his time was limited, his death imminent, and that he should do what he needed to do—which was put an end to all the problems of philosophy—as quickly as he could. He confessed to David Pinsent, his best friend at Cambridge, that he was painfully lonely, had been planning his suicide for years, and was ashamed that he was too cowardly to go through with it. In his journal, he wrote, "If suicide is allowed then everything is allowed. If anything is not allowed then suicide is not allowed. This throws a light on the nature of ethics, for suicide is, so to speak, the elementary sin. . . . Or is even suicide in itself neither good nor evil?"

In his family, suicide was not allowed, and after Hans and Rudi died, the air in the palace grew thinner and thinner, eventually creating such intolerable tension that Karl relented and permitted his youngest sons, Paul and Ludwig, to go to school. Although their years of tutoring had not prepared them, Ludwig still got to skip some grades, which is the only reason he avoided sharing a classroom with another famous Austrian, Adolf Hitler, who learned slowly and was held back. The Wittgenstein brothers, unused to dealing with other children, cultivated their solitude. It was familiar, comfortable, even if they sometimes found even their own company unbearable. ("Hell isn't other people," Ludwig wrote. "Hell is yourself.") A tall, gangly, stuttering rich boy, highly intelligent and delighted with himself for it, egotistical, uninterested in playing with his fellow children—he had to enjoy being alone.

I was solitary too, but for a very different reason. I had no personality. One time, some of my classmates told me so, which unsettled me so much that I ran home and repeated the revelation to my sister. I wanted reassurance, but instead of consoling me, Blanca piled on. "You don't!" she said accusatorily. "You just copy me."

After that, I took my grievance—the girls at school said this; Blanca said that—to my mother. She hated liars and hypocrites, and not even for her daughter would she risk insincerity. She said, "Your sister's got a point. You do copy her. You're her shadow," and went back to her book, not seeing that I was a recalcitrant shadow, a shadow with dreams, a shadow who wanted my own shape, weight, light, self!

When Ludwig Wittgenstein was teaching in a one-horse Austrian town, he attempted to gain the trust or admiration of a student by asking, "What have been the most important events in your life, for example, deaths, suicides, madnesses, or sicknesses?"

If I'd been the student, what would I have said to Mr. Wittgenstein? I could have brought up my siblings' horrible accident the day of my First Communion. During the party—my parents always went big for communions—Pablo and Blanca, horsing around, galloped right through the glass living-room door. Blanca severed two tendons in her hand, Pablo gashed his neck, and I passed out on seeing all the blood, leaving my poor mother to deal with a lifeless communicant, two badly hurt children, and all the alarmed guests. But my mother grew during moments of crisis, acquiring superhuman levels of capability, and she got my sister into emergency surgery at the Clínica Teknon before the end of the night, saving her hand. Pablo turned out to have a surface injury, not a slit throat. I slept over at a neighbor's, wracked with guilt. I was the only one of my classmates to have taken communion: the Church had switched the administration of the sacrament from seven to eight, but my sister took her first at seven, and I refused to fall behind her. After a stubborn campaign (I don't remember this, but according to my mother, I left every test at school blank, not dropping my strike until I'd achieved my goal), I prevailed in joining the communion class above mine, full of eight- and nine-year-olds. Imagine my seven-year-old pride as I marched down the nave with my candle that day! But God punished me. After that, it only took me a handful of years to free myself from Him. As for guilt . . .

I'm not sure what age I was—nine or ten—when my apartment caught fire, but I certainly would have told Ludwig about it: he was interested in calamities. It happened on an evening when Blanca and I, against very clear maternal orders, were messing around with a popcorn popper my godfather had given me. Suddenly smoke started surging through our room. We assumed it came from the forbidden machine, but when we unplugged it and the smoke, rather than dissipating, came faster and got denser, we got scared and went to tell our mother, who was in bed healing from a varicose-vein surgery, and by the time we'd gotten her to the bedroom, flames were already climbing out of the ceiling, where some circuit had blown. The next image I have is me, Blanca, and Pablo huddled on the upstairs neighbors' balcony as our apartment vomited ominous clouds of black smoke. On the street, a crowd of bystanders goggled at the three fire trucks and waved up at us, the victims, with fear and pity. (In the end, the flames ate my room and most of the hallway. Our whitewashed walls turned black, and for months after everything was repainted, we could still smell smoke, charred wood, and scorched plastic.) My mother ripped all her stitches, but she said nothing. She just dealt with the situation: evacuating us, calling 112, getting the firefighters inside and remaining in our home until they put the fire out.

It was then that my insomnia began. I couldn't sleep in my room. I was frightened of another fire. What if I died on the coals? At night, I got up and stood sentry at my parents' door, waiting to get up the courage or to be sick enough of lurking in the dark to knock and whisper, "Mamá, Mamá," hoping not to wake my dad.

"What's wrong?"

"I'm scared."

And my mother, who couldn't stand being woken, wrapped herself in a robe and came out of her room. I remember that. She didn't understand my anxiety—she was immune to fear—but she comforted me.

Here's another scene of my childhood: me and my siblings naked from the waist up, standing in line for a maid to whip us with a crop my father brought home as a souvenir. She did this every time my mother went out. When we told on her, my mom thought we were lying. For her, trusting her domestics over her children was a point of pride, and besides, she thought you should always listen to adults, since kids make things up. But one day she came home to see a crowd goggling at our balcony, just like the day of the fire, only this time the unhinged maid was straddling the railing, shrieking, "I'm going to jump! I'm going to jump!"

She didn't jump. My mom stopped her. She could handle any crisis, like I said.

Ludwig trains his big, serious gray eyes on me. He's disappointed that the girl didn't kill herself. He's sick of my stories. He's running out of patience.

"I have more," I inform him. "I have a story you'll like," and, before he can motion for me not to tell it, I start setting the scene.

It was a Sunday in winter, right around my fourteenth birthday. My mom was driving us home from a ski weekend in Formigal. We left after lunch, which we had not had together; she left us kids and went out with her friends. For all I know, she was happy and relaxed at the restaurant, but by the time she got back to our apartment, her mood had shifted. She rained shouts and threats upon us as we silently shoved our bags and gear into the old family Seat, hoping good behavior would mitigate her anger enough that we could follow our usual strategy for when she was drunk, which was to vanish. In the car, we were so busy trying to let her pretend she was alone that when she took a curve in the highway at startling speed, we said nothing. We said nothing when she accelerated into a hairpin turn. We could tell where this drive was going, but that fate was less frightening than the explosion of rage that would result from asking her to please slow down, and so what we thought would happen did: she sped around a tight bend so quickly the car toppled onto its side. We skidded toward the edge of the mountain, then back toward the rock face. As if in slow motion, the car spun on its own axis one, two, three times. I heard a horrible silence. Skis and bags whirled around me. I'm dead, I thought—but then the car came to a halt, still on its side, in the middle of the highway, and there I was, hardly scratched. My brother Pablo and cousin Juanma were alive, too, but my relief was ruined when I saw that the driver's seat was empty. My mother was under the car.

We shouted at her then. We screamed and screamed, but she

didn't respond. When a pickup appeared, we flagged it down and, with the driver and his passenger helping, managed to rescue her. One of them leaned down and announced, "She's breathing!" She was unconscious, not dead.

As a girl, I nurtured a fantasy in which one day, any day, maybe the very Sunday I was devoting to this daydream instead of my chores, the doorbell rang. From my room, I heard strange voices echoing down the hall, then the visitors coming in. My mother called, "Clara, where are you? Your real parents are here." I hurried to the foyer, thrilled to finally be reunited with my parents, who turned out to be a tall, ruddy, friendly American couple who never drank wine, whisky, or any other alcohol, only water and Coke. My sister—my fake sister—watched, consumed by jealousy, as I stuffed some clothes into a suitcase and said goodbye without sorrow or rancor to my fake mother, and then I jetted off to the United States with my real family.

I thought my mother hated me.

After she died, well into my adulthood, her friend Isabel told me a story about when she, her husband José María, and my parents were young and she'd just had her daughter. My parents came to meet the baby, and my mom, entranced, said, "I want a little girl just like her."

"We're having boys," my dad snapped. His punishment? Two girls in a row.

Imagine my mother's disappointment when I was born. She was very in love with her husband, and she knew how badly he wanted a son; having my sister, their first, was a letdown, and I, their second girl, was unforgivable. I can understand, now, how guilty and desolate my mother must have felt (and even as a child, I had the vague sense that I hadn't met expectations, that it would all be smooth sailing if I were a boy), and I can see how her shame could have led to the disinterest—it was almost dislike—with which she treated Blanca and me. My mother loved her sons and considered her daughters superfluous, a preference that was no secret: there's no doubt that she would've been happier without us. Ironically, her mother, my grandmother, passed her over for a boy, too. Until she was ten, my mom was the spoiled baby of her family, but she lost favor when her brother Tito was born. She resented my grandmother's conduct profoundly, and yet she reproduced it with us, and so it goes: as we age, we turn into our parents, falling into the habits, tics, and obsessions that once drove us insane. I, for instance, have slipped into my mother's vice: just like her, I spend my nights calling my friends and telling them how to live their lives. Unlike her, though, I don't get angry if they don't listen. I don't have her authority.

My sister and I were "the girls" until the day my mother died. It didn't matter that Blanca was married and had kids of her own. We were "the girls"; my brothers, "the boys." In his Tractatus, Wittgenstein explains that language creates pictures of reality. We say "boy" and a vision appears in our minds. Language and its correlates determine our perceptions of ourselves and our surroundings, such that "the limits of my language are the limits of my world."

Later, though, he retracted this idea in favor of the theory of language games. We can't have faith in words, he realized, when they all change meanings depending on use and context. Saying "boy" in a neutral voice isn't the same as an affectionate "my boy" or imperious "Boy!," and when my mother said "the boys," her tone and affect told you it meant something completely different from "the girls." When she said the latter, her eyes hardened, and you knew what she meant was "my enemies."

It was true. Starting in childhood, my sister and I were my mother's enemies. Our relationships with her were so awful that in our family, "the girls" meant "the Furies," "the witches," "the harpies," or else "bad," "unruly," "aggressive," and it's true that we were disobedient, and I suppose bad, too. Blanca, like any eldest child, fought my mother for her rights and freedoms, but their mutual loathing made every argument worse. I, the shadow, always sided with my sister. Maybe that's why my father thought I wasn't built for the law: good lawyers don't join a lost cause.

My father sold the family home several years ago, and, before he emptied it out for the move, invited us to come get our belongings, our memories. My brother Pablo got around to it before any of the rest of us, and reported that he'd gone in a closet and found, on a high shelf, papers our mother had saved from our childhoods. I thought of my earliest literary efforts, deranged parodies of my dime-store romances that I wrote to entertain my siblings and impress my mom, and got curious to reread them after so many years. At my father's house, I dragged a ladder into the closet and inspected the shelf, where I found nursery-school drawings, homework assignments, photo albums, and even college notes belonging to all three of my brothers, but not one scrap of paper Blanca or I had touched. It was as if my mother had wanted to erase us from the record. She'd tried to edit reality, to create a parallel universe in which she had no daughters, which I can understand. I forgive her. We gave her a lot of trouble. I did, anyway.

Marjorie Perloff, not that I know who she is, writes in her introduction to *Wittgenstein's Ladder*, which I found online, that in 1939,

> Ludwig Wittgenstein and his young Cambridge student and friend Norman Malcolm were walking along the river when they saw a newspaper vendor's sign announcing that the Germans had accused the British government of instigating a recent attempt to assassinate Hitler. When Wittgenstein remarked that it wouldn't surprise him at all if it were true, Malcolm retorted that it was impossible because "the British were too civilized and decent to attempt anything so underhand, and . . . such an act was incompatible with the British 'national character.'"

Wittgenstein was furious. Some five years later, he wrote to Malcolm,

> Whenever I thought of you I couldn't help thinking of a particular incident which seemed to me very important . . . you made a remark about "national character" that shocked me by its primitiveness. I then thought: what is the use of studying philosophy if all that it does for you is to enable you to talk with some plausibility about some abstruse questions of logic, etc., & if it does not improve your thinking about the important questions of everyday life, if it does not make you more conscientious than any . . . journalist in the use of the DANGEROUS phrases such people use for their own ends.

Ludwig was outraged that his disciple would speak of abstractions like "national character" without acknowledging their lack of substance and content. He considered "nation" and "homeland" *flatus vocis*, empty phrases, though when the First World War broke out, he joined the Austro-Hungarian Army as a private and fought without hesitation for his homeland and nation, impelled by the itch of obligation, another meaningless word.

I, too, distrust abstractions, and as a former lawyer, I'm repelled by rules. I'm disinterested in the novel as a unified form, preferring Cervantes's vision of it as an "unconfined way of writing," which suggests that a novel can accommodate anything, including chaos, so long as the author's working with purpose. Still, my conscience started intruding several pages ago, asking whether I really do have a purpose for these abrupt cuts from Sandra Mozarowsky to my mother, my mother to Wittgenstein, Wittgenstein to the king, the king to myself. Do I know where I'm going? Am I going anywhere? If so, why take such a circuitous route?

I'm doing my best to persuade myself that the game I'm inventing has logic and rules. Sandra was my age. Both of us studied ballet in childhood, though with different outcomes. She played the guitar, which I attempted to learn. She was half-Russian, and I'm obsessed with Russian literature. Her father was a diplomat from Yugoslavia, a country whose disintegration I wrote a novel about. Sandra told an interviewer she planned to study law in order to follow her dad into the foreign service, and when I was a law student, my dad tried unsuccessfully to persuade me to take the foreign-service exam ("You just want to get rid of me," I thought, "and I won't give you the satisfaction"). As for Wittgenstein, our mothers were named María Josefa, and he had an aunt named Clara. He was the black sheep of his family and I'm the black sheep of mine. His father died in his sleep and my mother died in bed. Otherwise, we've got nothing in common. Maybe that's one of this novel's rules: dissimilarity.

In 1906, when he was seventeen, Ludwig Wittgenstein enrolled at the Technische Hochschule of Charlottenburg to study mechanical engineering. After two years, he transferred to the University of Manchester for a PhD in aeronautics. He wanted to design a plane. His classmates, I imagine, thought of their flamboyant Austrian colleague as hypereducated but socially stunted, prone to outbursts of fury. He struggled to relate to normal people. He had no patience for their slow minds and imperfect comprehension. He only felt at home among rare intellects like his own, which is, surely, the curse of genius: not just loneliness, but the uneasy feeling of being a giant in Lilliput.

I wasn't repelled or annoyed by ordinariness. I was Wittgenstein's opposite: all I wanted was to be normal. I thought it was the only way I'd ever be happy. I remember going to my parents' house in Ciutadella de Menorca the summer before starting college, when I was eighteen. My parents had bought a house that once belonged to the diocese, and even after my mother renovated it, the lower level, a dark warren where servants and laborers had once lived and where my siblings and I now slept, was a labyrinth in which it was easy to get lost. My parents' room was upstairs, where the nobles had slept and where the prior owner, doña Eugenia, had her room, her parlor, and her chapel.

In my memory, it's a hot, humid night, and I'm sitting in

my cave: a vaulted, stone-walled room with a low ceiling and not one window. Judging by its battered stone water trough, it was designed to house animals. I'm smoking a joint and trying to read *Madame Bovary*, but all I can focus on is the heat, the mosquitoes, and the sensation that hours, minutes, *time* is sliding by and not a single thing is happening to me while my sister is laughing and whispering on the other side of the wall, which distracts and annoys me even more. *That*'s life, I tell myself: having fun with someone else. My sister is with her boyfriend Alejandro, who installed himself in her room two weeks ago. My mother has no idea. She never comes down here. She put in an intercom so she could summon us up.

I suck miserably on my joint. How can I weasel myself into other people's lives? Blanca has friends and a boyfriend. My mother has a jammed social calendar. Emma Bovary has all her lovers. What do I have? My whole life is limbo. As further torture, I tell myself my isolation is permanent, that I'm going to spend all my days alone in my room, reading and getting high. Eventually, around midnight or one, sick and afraid of my airless cave—did I mention it was full of flying cockroaches?—I wrap myself in my sheets and creep upstairs to my favorite room, the one decorated with kanthas, tapestries, and lamps my mother has brought back from trips to India. I fall asleep on one of the twin beds, still in my own sheets. No more than four hours later, my mother bursts in, shouting and shoving me out of the bed, outraged at my violation of the room.

My mother is very hospitable. She has guest rooms in all her homes, and in the Menorca one, she has four, which her children are forbidden from using when she has no guests. We're not worthy yet, and so she and I repeat this perverse scene every night. I fall asleep in the India room, and my mother comes in from some party or dinner or club and rousts me out. It's a strange sort of guerrilla war, one I don't know why I'm fighting. It's awful and painful to have my sleep interrupted daily by shouting, slaps, insults, an aggression that feels like hate, and yet I persist in provoking it. I keep going upstairs.

While researching propeller design, Wittgenstein got interested in the fundamentals of math. At the time, the leading authority was the British philosopher Bertrand Russell, whose *Principia Mathematica* demonstrated that math derives from the principles of logic. Wittgenstein headed to Cambridge, where Russell taught, and, on arriving, marched into Russell's rooms without warning and explained in his rudimentary English who he was and why he had come. Soon, he'd made himself Russell's shadow, a rebellious shadow who, rather than tagging happily along with the philosopher, wanted to walk beside him, no, ahead of him, no, to be the bright body and make *him* the furtive shadow.

Wittgenstein started going to Russell's sparsely attended classes (mathematical logic is exceptionally difficult), and, before long, dominated the discussions, not letting anybody else talk. He pestered Russell constantly with his philosophical doubts, turning up at his dinner table and in his rooms at night. Russell thought he was a freak and a pain in the ass. Probably to give himself a break, he sent Wittgenstein to study with one of Cambridge's greatest logicians, a Dr. Johnson. After one meeting, Wittgenstein said it had taken him less than an hour to determine that he had nothing to learn from the distinguished philosopher. Johnson, meanwhile, complained that his new student had spent their whole conversation lecturing him. But despite all Ludwig's rudeness, Russell eventually concluded that he was a genius. In a letter to his girlfriend, Lady Ottoline Morrell, he wrote, "I love him and feel he will solve the problems I am too old to solve."

Ludwig agreed. He critiqued and corrected his master without restraint. Eventually, he got Russell to abandon speculative philosophy, at which he felt only he, Wittgenstein, could succeed. Russell would later write to Lady Morrell: "His criticism, tho' I don't think you realised it at the time, was an event of first-rate importance in my life, and affected everything I have done since. I saw that he was right, and I saw that I could not hope ever again to do fundamental work in philosophy." Ludwig couldn't physically kill Karl, the oppressive father who had driven his brothers to suicide, but he had no trouble spiritually killing Bertrand Russell, his father in philosophy.

I'm proud to say that I never gave a professor reason to consider me annoying or intrusive. I never harassed them with ill-timed juridical doubts or attacked their ideas or informed them that my intellect outweighed theirs; I never turned up my nose at my coursework in civil law or administrative law or legal philosophy as Wittgenstein did when he eventually condescended to study the history of philosophy. He concluded, with his usual arrogance, that Plato, Aristotle, Aquinas, Hegel, and Kant were all full of shit. I, meanwhile, demonstrated exquisite tact at university. I was unsurpassed at not bothering my professors. In fact, I never even inconvenienced them with my presence.

My mother found this delicacy infuriating. She wanted me to go to class, not spend my days reading on the sofa (when she wasn't on it, that is). As counsel for the defense, I'd point out that on my first day of college, I headed right off to the

Universidad Central de Barcelona's law school at the corner of Diagonal and Pedralbes, a leisurely ten-minute walk from home. Our ninth-floor apartment, to which we moved from Sarriá when I was ten or eleven, was also on Pedralbes, which was not a minor influence on my decision to study law. Anyway, I went to school, but I was joined there by such a swarm of students that I couldn't get into the room. Our course was so oversubscribed it looked more like a protest than a class. Only the luckiest or most neurotic among us had arrived early enough to get seats. Others sat on the radiators, leaned on the walls, or spilled out into the hallway, craning and twisting and struggling to take notes. It was a mess, I told my mother at lunch. Complete disaster. Sure, the professor's lecture was great, but who could follow in a situation like that?

I went back the next day, not walking so leisurely this time. At precisely 9:00 A.M., I arrived at the faculty and found another throng of students, another overflowing room. As I remember, I showed up one more time, with the same results, and then abstained from attendance for the rest of my student career. I registered, I took my exams, and that was it. If I could have sat in my seat and read novels, I'd have gone to class daily—or maybe not. If truancy were allowed and teachers didn't take attendance, I doubt I'd have shown up at high school, either.

My first semester, I sent in the required photo with my registration forms, but after that, I didn't bother, which means the professors who graded my tests couldn't possibly have matched my face to my name. I was a ghost student, a shadow. Whereof one cannot speak, thereof one must remain silent, and I'm sure that if I ever came up, my professors had nothing to say.

"You just do what you want," my mother accused angrily

when she sat down with her breakfast at the dining table and found me in the living room, lying on her sofa with a book. She had a point. I, however, had a purpose, a method to my madness. I wanted to remedy my ignorance. My goal was to read everything, to learn what every word meant (as if a word had one static meaning!). Until then, I'd read without order, preferring nineteenth-century novels and contemporary literature to the classics (though I'd devoured Shakespeare's tragedies at fourteen; I couldn't get enough of his kings and princes, but I was such a snob that his aristocrat-less comedies didn't interest me). Now the time to educate myself had come. I was going to read Aristotle, Plato, Sophocles, Euripides, Homer, Virgil, Seneca, Petronius, Marcus Aurelius, the Archpriest of Hita, Fernando de Rojas, Don Juan Manuel, Garcilaso de la Vega, Fray Luis de León, San Juan de la Cruz, Lope, Calderón, Góngora, Quevedo, Cervantes of course, Dante, Petrarch, Rabelais, Voltaire, on and on. It was an arduous program, and I applied myself to it with discipline and tenacity I wish I still had.

"Why aren't you at school today?"

"I'm reading *Hume*, Ma."

I couldn't have said that. She just would have gotten madder. But it was her fault, in a way: I inherited my mania for reading from her. We had a good library at home, and she never prohibited me from reading a single book, though sometimes she'd say, "You won't like that." We didn't have a television until I was twelve. She thought it would make us read less and spend less time together. She wound up regretting it, at least where I was concerned.

My father, equally frustrated by having me lying around,

announced that I would be working in his office two afternoons a week, but his secretary, who was jealous of her responsibilities, wouldn't give me anything to do, which meant I could read free of maternal recriminations. Once my dad caught on, he gave me a tome of British bankruptcy law to translate into Spanish. It became my version of Laertes's shroud, shrinking as it grew, such that I wondered if the text turned back into English in the night. I never got it done.

I had one friend from school, Elisenda. (You try meeting people when you only show up to take tests.) She'd done the university orientation course with me, and she told me when the exams were and let me borrow her notebooks. If she couldn't help, I sucked it up and went to campus, where I asked the more diligent students to let me copy their work, or, if they weren't forthcoming, trudged to a print shop where an enterprising future lawyer let you Xerox his for a fee; notes secured, I took the metro to the part of the Rambla that used to be Chinatown and bought hash from an androgynous dealer at Bar Pitirirí on Calle San Ramón, and once I was fully supplied with drugs, notes, and textbooks, I studied—and oh, did I study! All day and half the night, I pored over the syllabus, learning each lecture by heart so that I could, as expected, regurgitate it on the exam, not even skipping the jokes. On the day of the test, I'd turn to my neighbor and hiss, "What's our professor named?" so I could put the right information in my header. By the next day, I'd have forgotten what the exam said.

In my family, the rules were clear. Our only obligation was to pass our classes. Ideally, we'd get straight As. I attacked and defeated my tests, which made my mother feel impotent. She couldn't force me to go to school if I held up my end of the bargain. Still, she had the sense that I'd tricked her, even though I was following the rules.

Ludwig spent the summer of 1913 vacationing in Norway with David Pinsent, a promising young mathematician who happened to also be a very handsome young man. Wittgenstein paid for first-class travel and five-star hotels, but Pinsent still struggled with his friend's insistence on wrestling with logic problems in the mornings and his tendency to react to Pinsent's interests in photography and chatting with strangers by going from calm to furious silence. Pinsent wasn't sure why: jealousy? A general disregard for humanity? Still, Wittgenstein said it was the best trip of his life.

On his return, Ludwig sent Bertrand Russell an urgent summons, saying he'd had a transcendent revelation. When Russell came, Wittgenstein informed him, "A is the same as A."

After that, he decided he'd exhausted Cambridge. He returned to Norway and sequestered himself in a cabin on an isolated fjord so he could progress in his investigations. Russell said he'd lost his mind. Ludwig agreed. Pinsent, hurt by his departure, never saw him again. Wittgenstein didn't re-enter society for a year, emerging from his isolation only because his mother was very sick. Karl had died already, and so Poldy's death made Wittgenstein a multimillionaire. He wasn't happy about it. Money unsettled him. He had no idea what to do with it, and possessing it distracted him from his goal of understanding the truth. He dabbled in anonymous patronage, funding young poets like Rilke and Trakl, but he neither read their work nor wanted to, and keeping them afloat hardly diminished his wealth.

When World War I started in July 1914, he still found himself in Vienna. He wished to return to England, but it was no longer possible. He had a double hernia that would have exempted him from military service, but his sense of duty made him enlist as a private. Years later, he'd say, "Nowadays it is the fashion to emphasize the horrors of the last *war*. I didn't find it so *horrible*." He also claimed, "The *war saved my life*. I don't know what I would have done without it." According to his sister Hermine, he joined up not out of patriotic ardor, but to get absorbed in something difficult enough to keep his attention off his intellectual work.

Wittgenstein was of the opinion that war teaches us about human nature and the meaning of life ("only death gives life its meaning," he wrote). He accepted the rigors of training enthusiastically, submitting to military discipline. Sent to the navy, he set sail on the *Goplana*, a captured Russian boat that patrolled the Vistula. His job was operating the searchlight.

David Pinsent, with whom Ludwig was secretly in love, tested planes for the Royal Air Force. (Amid the carnage, the war was a battle of gentlemen: Pinsent congratulated Wittgenstein on joining the enemy side.) Bertrand Russell committed himself to pacificism. He opposed the war publicly, agitating so loudly and insistently for peace that he got thrown in jail. During the war, Russell abandoned all philosophical activity. Wittgenstein, who fought, did not. (On returning to Cambridge after the Armistice, he went to a meeting of the League for Peace and Freedom to tease Russell. "I suppose you would prefer a League for War and Slavery," said Russell, and Wittgenstein shot back, "Much rather, much rather!")

During the war, he recorded his activities in a notebook,

which is the reason we know he bought Tolstoy's *Gospel in Brief* at a store in Tarnów where there was no other book to buy. It impressed him profoundly, invigorating his relationship to Christianity and conferring a mystical tone on his diary entries. He frequently invoked God and prayed for strength to bear the cross not of rigid naval discipline or icy night watches, not of the ship's poor hygiene or grim cuisine, no, Ludwig suffered from the "stupidity, insolence, and malice of this bunch," meaning the other sailors on the *Goplana*. His comrades frequently went on benders, which appalled the puritanical Ludwig. He tried unsuccessfully to "practice complete passivity," and spent his nights manning the searchlight and afternoons peeling potatoes, an activity that relaxed him enough to dedicate his mind to his one true calling: mathematical logic. Every so often he masturbated, which he recorded punctiliously in his diary alongside the formula "aRB.aRc.bSc - aR(bSc) Def. (GT1, s5)."

He was sure his comrades hated him for having volunteered rather than getting conscripted. I'm sure his disdain, snobbery, and reserve didn't help. If I'd been on the *Goplana*, hungry and louse-bitten and tired of saluting all the time, I would have wanted to get drunk with my friends, to release my unhappiness for a while, to make fun of that arrogant dick Wittgenstein who thought he was so great for enlisting, who turned up his nose at us, who—have you heard?—was a multimillionaire. Hiding from us in his cabin, Ludwig writes, "Night before last, terrible scenes: practically everyone drunk," and prays, "If this is the end for me, may I die a good death, worthy of my best self. May I never lose my self."

Now Ludwig is in a packed, smoky club with deafening music and strobe lights that make him feel sick. "Get up (get on up) / Stay on the scene (get on up) like a sex machine"—my song! I hurl myself at the dance floor the second I hear its opening groove. I'm no sex machine myself, but I live in hope. "Wait a minute! Shake your arm, then use your form / Stay on the scene like a sex machine." I try my hardest: wiggle my ass, thrust my hips, wave my arms, oh, how I dance!

"You're a terrible dancer," Ludwig says.

"I know," I tell him, "but I don't care. I'm rolling. You can't blame me. I'm like the king: not liable for my actions. And I came here to be out of control, anyway. I'm here to lose myself, get a *new* self, be outgoing and flirty and brave. You know, I'm good at picking up men now. I can just look at one—see, like that!—and I bet he'll come over. I'm not ashamed. I have friends now. I'm normal, I'm having fun, and I love everyone, even you, but I have to go. I just saw the guy I buy ecstasy from, and I want some more before I start coming down."

"Fix your skirt," Ludwig scolds. "It's sideways."

Aboard the *Goplana* Wittgenstein carried out his duties, marched forward in logic, and waited impatiently to hear from his beloved Pinsent (from whom I'm still shocked he got letters mid-war), but he still worried he'd abandoned himself to an easy, comfortable lifestyle. He considered life "an intellectual problem and a moral requirement," and felt that he could only carry out the latter if he went to the front. Only then, he wrote, "will the war begin for me. And—possibly—life too! Perhaps nearness to death will bring light into my life. May God enlighten me."

His wish comes true. He's sent to Polish Galicia, the Eastern front, as a scout in the 4th Battalion of the 5th Austro-Hungarian regiment. A new notebook begins. Only this fragment remains from his entry on March 28th, 1916: ". . . and must take my life. I suffered the tortures of hell! And yet the picture of life was so enticing to me that I wanted once more to live. I will take poison only when I really want to poison myself." In other entries, he urges himself on, writing, "You must do your best. You cannot do more: and be of good cheer. Be satisfied with yourself" (a goal he never achieved). On April 6th, he writes, "I was sick. Today still very weak. Today my commander said he would have me sent to the interior, away from the Front. If that happens, I will kill myself," but that Saturday, April 15th, his outlook has improved: "We will be at the Front in 8 days. May it be granted to me to put my life in play by receiving a difficult assignment!"

But the front lets him down. He's not in enough danger. He requests a transfer to an observation post that's constantly exposed to enemy fire. Once there, he writes, "I'm like the prince in the enchanted castle. Now all is quiet during the day, but at night there must be terrible things going on! Will I be able to stand it????"

He comported himself heroically. His commander at the Battle of Okna, in recommending him for the Silver Medal of Valor, wrote, "Volunteer Wittgenstein was attached to the Observer officer during the engagements . . . from 4-6 vi 16. Ignoring the heavy artillery fire on the casement and the exploding mortar bombs he observed the discharge of the mortars and located them. The Battery in fact succeeded in destroying two of the heavy-caliber mortars by direct hits, as was confirmed by prisoners taken. On the Battery Observation Post . . . he observed without intermission in the drumfire, although I several times shouted to him to take cover." Wittgenstein received the medal and was promoted to sergeant.

We courted danger, too. We risked our lives, though all we wanted was to have fun. Borges said that writers shouldn't try to be modern; that it happens by virtue of living in the present. I disagree. You can live a whole life outside the present day. I would know. Under Franco, Spain felt that we occupied a different time than our neighbors. Our clock had stopped at some point after the war. We had a dictator who wouldn't die and an ocean and mountain range cutting us off from the lucky countries who'd been living in the future for decades. We envied the Europeans wholeheartedly, and agreed with their assessment that we, the Spanish, were a backward nation living in the past.

After we got democracy, politics was no longer the main reason we didn't sleep. My generation now had another urgent responsibility: leaping into the future. It only took us a few years to earn global praise for our frantic, furious modernity. European media was all over our music, our art, the whole Movida Madrileña. Spain surprised the whole globe. It was miraculous: a cabinet of Francoist ministers who'd smothered protests with bullets suddenly transformed into beacons of democracy!

In my childhood, women, my mother included, wore veils and cardigans to Mass. Such was life under Franco: covering up, hiding ourselves. No wonder we went so wild—and fought so much—about *destape*, dumb as it was. And look at me just a few years after Franco died, sunbathing nude on a Menorcan beach with a pair of friends, one naked like me, the other shielded by a long-sleeved shirt with the cuffs buttoned around her wrists. Nudity was my cause then. I felt that exhibiting my body affirmed my new freedom. Sure, it was still illegal, but that made it even more necessary. In fact, that made it my duty.

A family arrives at the beach and glowers their condemnation at us. "Sluts!" they hiss. "Degenerates!" All the adults mutter about our shamelessness, and the littlest girl tosses stones at us. We ignore them. We act as if we're alone, as if we hear nothing, as if the pebbles don't hurt. We're engaged in a war between the future (represented by us) and the past (represented by the family, but also by Franco), and we have faith that the past will get sick of harassing us. I hardly slept last night, and eventually, I fall asleep in the sun.

My non-naked friend wakes me up. She points at the dune behind us. A pair of cops are jogging toward the beach, trailed by the family's teenage daughter, who, evidently, was sent to get them. Her satisfied parents waste no time in denouncing us, shouting, "It's them!," but the police can't accuse us of shamelessness now: we're in the water, covered to our necks by the sea. All the agents can do is park themselves on the shore and watch us, clutching their guns. Sun glitters on their mirrored glasses. Sweat from their run is probably trickling under their olive uniforms, their wide belts, their regulation boots. We smile defiantly at them, prepared to remain in the water until they abandon their post. Our clothed friend waves at us from the beach to bolster our spirits. If we give up and get out, the cops will catch us in flagrante delicto and we'll spend the night in jail.

Hours pass. No longer interested in us, the upstanding family gathers their belongings and leaves the beach. So does the sun. We're not smiling any more. A cell is beginning to seem preferable to the frigid darkness of the sea . . . But then, with no warning, the cops turn and trudge up the dune without looking back. Our friend is finally alone on the shore with our bags and towels. We emerge from the water, hypothermic but victorious, and she greets us with jittery relief. It wasn't shame or prudery that made her keep her shirt on. She's got track marks. She's afraid to let anyone see the ominous trail of dark lines on her veins, and now she's in a poorly concealed hurry to get back. We don't ask why. No need.

"He who is happy must have no fear. Not even of death," writes Wittgenstein. "Only he who lives, not in time but in the present, is happy. For life in the present there is no death. Death is not an event in life. We do not live through it in the world." We were happy. Our life was a continuous party, and while you're on a dance floor or in a mosh pit, when you've got shots and lines to do, you don't have a care in the world. Not while the music's playing—but every so often, we unplugged the sound system. In daylight, we had other faces, other demeanors. We greeted each other with a certain embarrassment, a sudden discomfort, stiff in our unfamiliar, formal clothes. We hardly recognized each other, and we had no idea what to say, consumed as we were by our anxiety and preoccupation with who would go next.

In the homily, the priest was discreet and tactful. He assured us that our beloved brother had died a Christian death and was now resting in the peace of God. We wanted to believe him. It would have been nice to imagine our friend dressed as a cherub, playing the harp with the angels, but we all knew he'd been found in the bathroom with a needle hanging from his arm.

And so the eighties went, a decade of parties and funerals, the parties shrinking in size and the funerals growing in number every year. My boyfriend at the time would sometimes say,

"You're so beautiful. I love you so much," and snuggle his head on my shoulder. I'd take his face in my hands and peer into his eyes to see if his pupils were reduced to points, if his eyelids were drooping, if a soft smile was flickering on his mouth (the only state in which he was so sweet to me).

I'd get mad then. "You can't even see me!," I'd say, but of course he denied it. Junkies default to lying. Every family had one: a self-absorbed, infuriating addict who stole and cheated, whose days hinged on secretive phone calls, who retreated like Kubla Khan into a solitary pleasure-dome. An addict was gone even when he was there. He scratched his face, shut his eyes, let his happiness stream from his lips, gone even when he was saying he loved you so much and you were so beautiful.

Addicts became Public Enemy #1. Spooked journalists reported nonstop on this plague: overdoses, AIDS, not what we'd signed up for. Nobody warned us. We just wanted to have fun.

"We're not here to enjoy ourselves!" Ludwig says.

Slowly we caught on. We who'd bragged about being transgressive, even revolutionary, surprised ourselves by falling into routines and going to work just like the parents we scorned. I put on my pantsuits and played lawyer. Camus wrote, "Rising, street-car, four hours in the office or the factory, meal, street-car, four hours of work, meal, sleep, and Monday Tuesday Wednesday Thursday Friday and Saturday according to the same rhythm—this path is easily followed most of the time," but it was a struggle for me.

Look at me now, a public defender in a police station, helping a girl much younger than me give a statement. She's only twenty-two, though she looks aged to her bones. Welts mar her face and neck. Her hair is a dirty mess, and her ratty clothes droop from her limbs. She tells the cop, tells me, that the two thousand pesetas found on her person are "legal earnings from prostitution."

At his typewriter, the policeman pauses to look at her disdainfully. "No one's going to screw you. You're disgusting."

He goes back to typing. I can't deny his point: the girl gives me the creeps. She may have been a prostitute once, but now she's a pickpocket who steals purses and wallets from tourists and one poor immigrant who had nothing but his return ticket to Nigeria and who pointed her out to the cops. She has four children and a "husband" dying of AIDS in a prison hospital.

"How many times have you been arrested?" the cop asks.

"Counting today, three," says my client.

"Counting today, *twenty*-three," he corrects.

Usually, a person under arrest sits beside the desk of the officer taking their statement, but he's put the girl's chair several meters away, which means we're constantly raising our voices and mishearing each other. After the statement is done, all three of us sign it. My client, like all my clients after arrests, asks me for money and tobacco. I give her cigarettes and a handshake, but not cash.

"How can you touch her?" demands the cop, horrified. "Can't you see she has AIDS?" I say goodbye, extending my hand.

In all probability, the judge who sentences this girl will condemn a dead woman. All my state clients are seropositive addicts. I can't give them anything but cigarettes. Ludwig was far more generous. He gave away his massive fortune.

He was sent to the Italian front with an artillery regiment in 1918. He saw that the war was ending, that his side was losing, that his fellow Austro-Hungarian officers were fleeing, abandoning their sleepwalking army, but not Ludwig. It would have contravened his moral code. After being captured by the Allies, he awaited the armistice in a prison camp where he completed his magnum opus, which he would title *Tractatus Logico-Philosophicus.*

He went home to Vienna, where he learned that David Pinsent had died in an aviation accident and his brother Kurt had committed suicide in a trench. According to Camus, "the most important thing you do every day you live is deciding not to kill yourself," an aphorism Ludwig incarnated. He debated suicide, which he felt was his fraternal duty, the ultimate demonstration of gallantry. Discouraged by his failure to die, he scolded himself for his weakness. His family fretted about his sanity. His behavior got odder and odder, and he devoted himself to getting rid of his money. (I'm not surprised his siblings thought he'd lost it. I can't understand him either. "Ludwig," I'd say, "you were born with a silver spoon in your mouth. You have no idea. I've pawned my baptism jewelry, my Communion jewelry. I had to pawn my gold tooth!")

I was broke. Ludwig wanted to be. He split his vast fortune not among the humble and unlucky but among his siblings, already millionaires.

> The world is everything that is the case.
> The world is the totality of facts, not of things.
> The world is determined by the facts, and by
> these being all the facts.
> For the totality of facts determines both what is
> the case, and also all that is not the case.

So opens the *Tractatus Logico-Philosophicus*, which Wittgenstein dedicated to David Pinsent. He managed his prepublication nerves by declaring that no one could understand it, including Russell, who offered to lend his name to the book by writing an introduction (Wittgenstein was just some Austrian; Russell, the world's most celebrated philosopher). Ludwig accepted ungraciously, but, on reading his affectionate mentor's text, he rejected it and wrote his own prologue, highlighting a point that Russell had failed to notice: the *Tractatus* was the "final solution to the problem of philosophy." His effort to render all present and future philosophers jobless concludes with this enigmatic phrase: "Whereof one cannot speak, thereof one must remain silent."

Per Ludwig, his predecessors in philosophy had erred by discussing the unspeakable. Such subjects, he said, fall outside the logic of language and rules of silence. Still, these are the most important ideas there are: divinity (or its absence), good, evil, beauty, sentiment, emotion, Chekhov's "real, most interesting life." Now I'm waiting with Ludwig for the bathroom at some house party in Ensanche that neither of us was invited to (I tagged along with some friends of the host's friends). I'm holding a plastic cup of liquor in my right hand, my purse in my left. In my mouth is a cigarette that badly needs ashing. Its smoke irritates Ludwig. So do the loud partygoers, the booming music.

"What are you doing with yourself?" he asks. "Haven't you realized that life is an intellectual problem and a moral requirement? You're not a girl. You're nearly thirty. I'd solved all the problems of philosophy by your age," he reminds me, humble as ever. I remind him modestly that I won my case this week.

I'm not comparing us, but—Jesus, whoever's in the bathroom needs to hurry it up.

"All you do is get drunk, get high, and go dancing," he accuses. "It's a sin. Your life is false and unreasonable. You just eat, drink, and sleep. You're like an animal."

"Sure," I say. "I'm an insect. I'm a fly looking for the way out of a fly bottle."

"That's my line!" he says, getting mad, and I start telling him nobody cares when the bathroom door finally opens and two strangers emerge, laughing and rubbing their noses. Before Ludwig can jump ahead of me, I'm locking myself in, avoiding the mirror, digging out a baggie and bill and ID to cut a line, flushing the toilet while I'm bent over the tank so that Ludwig won't judge me even more than he already has, and I do know he has a point: I'm aging, my party spirit is flagging, and my confidence is getting a little forced, as is my conviction that it's transgressive to get drunk or high on Saturday nights (something only a child of dictatorship could ever have thought to begin with); what I really want, and want to tell Ludwig—in fact, what I'm *going* to tell him—is to talk about the very subjects he says philosophers should shut up about, the unspoken ones, which are the ones that matter. Alight with cocaine euphoria and ready to confront him, I open the bathroom door.

Sisyphus's punishment is also his salvation. If he summited the mountain and set his boulder down, freeing himself of its weight, then what would he do?

After publishing the final text in philosophical history, Ludwig got a gardening job at a monastery. You can't teach plants math, though, and it was against his perfectionistic morals to not aid his fellow man—in a vague, diffuse way, of course, since goodness is outside logic. He decided his mission was enlightening the ignorant. He was going to be a teacher.

He selected a godforsaken Austrian village of two hundred called Trattenbach, where he could live in the poverty and austerity his frugal, spartan soul required. He used a false name, since no one would have understood a Wittgenstein toiling in a rural high school. It would have seemed ridiculous, frivolous, which, in a way, it was. Rumors quickly swirled around him, fed by his exaggerated conduct and misanthropy. He got along poorly with his colleagues and scorned the whole town. ("I am still at Trattenbach," he wrote Russell, "surrounded, as ever, by odiousness and baseness. I know that human beings on the average are not worth much anywhere, but here they are much more good-for-nothing and irresponsible than elsewhere.") Although enthusiastic about teaching, he was not just hard on his students but infuriated by their dullness. He caned them, or pulled the girls' hair and the boys' ears, when they failed to follow his explanations of math.

He didn't last long in Trattenbach. He moved to nearby Hassbach, where the townspeople, he said, were "not human at all but loathsome worms." After a month with the worms, he tried his luck in the town of Otterthal, where he wrote a dictionary for children, the only text other than the *Tractatus* that he published in his life.

In April 1926, a tragedy occurred. Josef Haidbauer, the eleven-year-old son of a widow, so frustrated Wittgenstein with his limited gifts that the teacher hit him hard enough to knock him out. (A week earlier, Wittgenstein had pulled Josef's classmate Hermine Piribauer's ears until blood came out.) Our World War I hero left his victim in the principal's office and ran. The police chased and caught him; he was tried, subjected to psychological tests, but he was a Wittgenstein. His family made it go away.

"Hail Mary, full of grace."

"When did you last confess?" asked the priest behind his lattice.

"A week ago," I lied, and so my confession began.

As a girl, I went to Mass on Sundays with my family. My father left us outside the Church of the Salesians of Sarriá and headed to the Mokay Bar in Plaza Artós for a snack—it was a given that Mass was for women, children, and the elderly—and in the church, once my sister and I had confessed and received communion, we chased and harangued our brother Pablo until he did, too ("Pablo, you have to confess"; "Mamá, Pablo won't confess"; "*Ma,* tell him to confess!"). After that, we could reunite with our father and enjoy our own snacks, or tease the pigeons, or throw them French fries. It was an idyllic way to spend a Sunday.

Although the Wittgensteins were originally Jewish, their parents, like ours, raised them Catholic. Had Ludwig been my brother, I wouldn't have needed to heckle him into the confessional. He loved it. He confessed to himself in writing, raking over his life, dissecting each event to see how he should have behaved, what the correct reactions would have been in every circumstance. His goal wasn't to purge guilt. He wanted to humiliate himself in order to "remove a barrier, as it were, that stood in the way of an honest and decent thought," a project so vital to him—his motto was "understand or die"—that if he had an urgent need to confess, he'd turn anyone into the priest.

After sitting through a midnight confession, one of his Cambridge friends and disciples demanded, "What's wrong with you? Do you want to be perfect?"

"Of course I do!" Ludwig replied.

My priest asked, "What are your sins?"

"I disobeyed my parents, I fought with my sister, I said bad words, and I have a messy room." I always confessed the same sins; I never told the Father I'd been stealing grapes from a vineyard. It was none of his business.

Ludwig confessed to his friend Fania Pascal that he was Jewish, more Jewish than was widely known. He'd let people believe that he was three-quarters Aryan, one Jewish, when in fact he had three Jewish grandparents (though all were practicing Protestants) and one Aryan Catholic one. Wittgenstein had long been a self-hating Jew, an antisemite, really (he wrote that the Jewish mind was incapable of creation or invention, that the Jew could show talent but lacked genius: he himself, he said, was an example of this), but the persecution of Jews in Hitler's Germany shifted his thinking. He didn't confess to Fania Pascal that he was gay. Whereof one cannot speak . . .

It must have been the summer I was twenty-two, or maybe twenty-three. My friends and I were wandering near the Ciutadella port in Menorca around two or three in the morning, and the streetlamps' old, livid glow caught a shape I knew coming toward us. She was struggling uphill, stumbling, weaving, grumbling inaudibly as drunks do; she seemed defenseless, lost, alone.

I should have taken her arm. I should have said softly, "Come on, Ma. Let's go home." But I didn't. When our paths crossed, I turned my face and kept walking. If I had intercepted her, if

I'd tried to help, she'd have snatched her arm back and told me to leave her alone—and yet.

In 1936, ten years after the Otterthal incident, Wittgenstein returned to the town. He visited his old students' houses to ask forgiveness for his excesses. Josef Haidbauer was dead, but he found Hermine Piribauer still holding her grudge, as well as some less resentful students who accepted his apologies gracefully. It was an act of tremendous courage, and yet I doubt Wittgenstein truly longed for his victims to forgive him (forgiving someone is an act of generosity on the part of the offended; it doesn't redeem the offender). My guess is that he hoped his voluntary and deliberate humiliation would help him pardon or even absolve himself, erase his guilt, but only God can do that, and once you've killed God, why confess?

The Haidbauer scandal freed the children of Austria from Wittgenstein's lessons. He quit teaching and threw himself into designing a mansion in Vienna for his sister Gretl, a project that, due to the philosopher-architect's relentless perfectionism, took years: he had the ceiling of a room raised three centimeters after it was completed and took eternities choosing the materials, the radiators, the shape of every doorknob and handle. Meanwhile, the members of the Vienna Circle, an anti-metaphysical group of philosophers, got their hands on his *Tractatus* and dared to use it to justify logical posivitism, a new philosophical trend claiming science was the only true form of knowledge. They hadn't understood a thing! You couldn't *do* philosophy after the *Tractatus*! And besides, Wittgenstein was wary of science; he thought the Scientific Revolution augured the end of humanity. In order to discredit his followers, he made a drastic decision, something no philosopher had ever done before: he retracted his work. He announced publicly that the *Tractatus* was a failure. He kicked the boulder he'd tried so hard to haul up the mountain and sent it tumbling down.

Camus thought comprehending the absurd causes a break with the inertia of habit, but maybe he got it backward. Understanding the futility of life motivates us to create our own order, routines, repetitions, and rules that generate an illusion of purpose, of a path that leads somewhere. Wittgenstein succumbed to this temptation. He convinced himself he was obligated to return to philosophy, though he counseled his students to quit their useless discipline in favor of something serious, like carpentry. He returned to the Cambridge philosophy department, having admitted his error and accepted that he once more had to (got to) trudge up the mountain with his stone.

He was diagnosed with prostate cancer in 1950 and refused treatment. He didn't want to die in a hospital, and his physician, Edward Bevan, offered his house. On the night of April 28th, nursed by Edward's wife Joan Bevan, Ludwig reached his last moments. Before dying, he said, "Tell them I've had a wonderful life."

A few weeks before dying, my mother declared, "I've had a good life." We'd just eaten and were drinking coffee in the living room. She'd just had the flu, and was lying under a blanket on her sofa, which I no longer fought her for; it had been a long time since I lived at home. My father sat in one armchair, and I sprawled in the other. Dusky amber light trickled through the curtains, somehow matching my mother's relaxed, contented smile.

"I don't mind if I die," she said peaceably, not addressing either of us. It was as if she were speaking to the air. "I've lived enough." A moment later, she added, "I've had a good life."

Her declaration startled me. It was completely unanticipated, maybe because her life had never struck me as a good one, but she made a generous, sanguine assessment of her existence. My mother and Wittgenstein! You couldn't imagine two more different minds, and yet they reached the exact same conclusion: I'm not going to complain. My lot was good. Life was worth it.

I doubt Sandra Mozarowsky would have said the same thing.

CHAPTER 4

WITTGENSTEIN LIKED DETECTIVE FICTION, which he read to take breaks from his intense ruminations. For a philosopher whose goal was explaining all earthly problems through logic, it was surely gratifying to read a story that presents an enigma—a murder or murders, usually—then proceeds according to the rules of causality, using deduction to dismiss red herrings, gather evidence, investigate suspects and alibis, until the solution (i.e., murderer) is found and the mystery (i.e., motive) is resolved. Crime novels have a who, a why, a how. But what about a detective story about a death with no explanation, one that could have been an accident, a suicide, or a murder (but if it was, who's the murderer? What's the motive?), one that leaves the enigma in place? A story like that would be a joke, a rip-off, a failure you couldn't even turn into a B-movie starring Sandra Mozarowsky.

"Death will come and will bear your eyes," wrote Pavese, a cry in the night, a crash, a body on the sidewalk, a barefoot woman in just a kimono, bleeding . . .

"Sandra Mozarovsky hovers between life and death. She plunged from the balcony of her home and remains in a coma. Precise causes of the accident unknown," announces the headline of a report by Pilar Ferrer in the September 10, 1977, issue of *¡Hola!* In the lede Ferrer writes, "The actress's father declares, 'My daughter had no reason to jump,' rejecting insistent rumors about attempted suicide." The opening paragraph clarifies: "18-year-old Sandra Mozarowsky, an actress with more than ten roles to her name, a rising star of the new Spanish cinema, has hovered between life and death in the intensive care unit at the Ciudad Sanitaria Francisco Franco since very early on the morning of the 24th. She seems to have plunged from the balcony of the fourth-floor apartment she shares with her parents and siblings at 3 Calle Álvarez de Baena."

What makes a jump different from a fall? Jumping always means falling. A jump is a physical impulse up or down, followed by a descent, a fall, but it's also an act of will, a decision made by the jumper, even if it's a hopeless flight from a house in flames. A fall, not so much. Falling is passive. A person falls after slipping or stumbling or getting pushed. Its connotations are negative; its synonyms are "disgrace," "decadence," "decline." Jumping, on the other hand—well, Lucifer was the fallen angel, not the angel who jumped. "She plunged," meanwhile, is a cautious, ambiguous locution, one that refuses to take sides. You can plunge after either a jump or a fall.

Ángel negro was Sandra Mozarowsky's last movie (or Mozarovski or Mozarowski: her name appears all three ways). *Fotogramas* judges it a "very average melodrama that spices up a tale of vengeance with the requisite dose of eroticism that the moment (1977) seemed to demand. A Mexican-Colombian-Spanish coproduction, it has all the worst hallmarks of popular cinema descended from the photo novel, and its attempt to be cosmopolitanism does nothing but embarrass the viewer."

A tough assessment, yes, but fair. Still, *Ángel negro* has its charms, which are the same as its vicissitudes. Its international casting (it stars Carlos Ballesteros, Mónica Randall, and Sandra Mozarowsky, all Spanish; Jorge Rivero, Mexican; and Lyda Zamora, Colombian) has an unintentionally comic effect. Although it's set and shot in Colombia and all the characters are meant to be Colombian, only Lyda Zamora has that country's typical lilt: Jorge Rivero's pronunciation is as Mexican as ever, Sandra and Carlos Ballesteros have Madrid accents, and Mónica Randall speaks with a gentle Catalonian undertone. As for the visual effects, I'm not sure whether I should blame the terrible quality of the old VHS I ordered online, the distorting tendencies of my misconfigured television, or the cinematography, but the actors' legs are all shortened significantly, which adds to the unintentional comedy of the film, which is a deranged retelling of the Electra story in which Sandra plays the daughter of a rich Colombian architect (Carlos Ballesteros) and his wife (Mónica Randall), whose drug use is destroying her family. Sandra adores her elegant, upstanding father in a way that, in their scenes together, seems quasi-incestuous. He decides to check his degenerate wife into rehab against her wishes. One night, Sandra comes home from clubbing and witnesses her father's murder: an unseen hand (only Sandra, not the viewer, knows who it belongs to) stabs him in the throat with a pair of scissors, killing him and rendering Sandra, the witness, catatonic and then mute, an event that allows her to perform her usual scene, writhing in bed in her white blouse, expression vacant, eyes possessed. On her return to herself, she says she remembers nothing, which is the start of a plotline worthy of Machiavelli. Sandra, the avenging angel, masterminds a scheme that requires her to fake love for her mother and seduce her father's secretary, a lesbian gambling addict, as well as her young stepfather, a beefy ladies' man played by Jorge Rivero. She manipulates them cold-bloodedly until the moment arrives to take her revenge. On the way, there's blood, betrayal, vendetta, various pornographic detours in which breasts are everywhere and Sandra does full-frontal nudity. She does a good job. She turns her ridiculous role into something nearly believable, which can't have been easy and which suggests that she really would have been a good actress someday.

She died three weeks after her fall, on September 14th, 1977, without ever regaining consciousness. I have no memory of these events. Sandra Mozarowsky was not yet (and would never be) a famous actress, and since my mother didn't read tabloids, the only publications that reported on her state, we didn't have them in our house. In the twenty-one-day interim between her fall and her death, while she was in a coma, *¡Hola!*, *Pronto*, *Garbo*, *Lecturas*, *Semana*, and their peers echoed each other's claims and revelations about her. They got interviews with her family, or with her physician Dr. Llauradó, formerly the Generalissimo's doctor, who divulged that she fell sideways, landing on her head and back, and suffered a "major cranial trauma and four broken lower ribs, as well as several more fractures throughout her body." They generated hypotheses to explain what they all agreed was a "strange accident." A few of them suggested vaguely that depression, caused by taking "pills," could have led Sandra to commit suicide, but the most widely disseminated version, the one that prevailed in becoming official, was that she got vertigo while watering the plants on her balcony. Its cause: her obsession with losing weight. In the months before Sandra died, she'd gained some pounds, then gone on a very strict diet. She was also on a medicine that made her faint frequently, according to her parents and to sources identified as "someone close to the family." (Doctors were generous with amphetamines then: you could always get Bustaid, Centramina, or Minilip to help drop a kilo or two.) According to a *Semana* report promising to "reconstruct the facts," though, Sandra's mother said her daughter had "issues with her cervical vertebrae that her doctor was treating with antirheumatic drugs," and made no mention of amphetamines.

Our "reconstruction of the facts," done by someone with the byline M. V., claims,

> Sandra Mozarowsky went to the movies with her father on Tuesday the 23rd. Her mother remained at home, watching *Esta noche fiesta* on television until Sandra and her father returned. She [Sandra] changed into a kimono and went to water her plants on the balcony. Her father warned her not to go out without shoes. When she watered, she often leaned too far over the railing so she wouldn't get the downstairs neighbors' balcony wet, which meant exposing her body too much.
>
> Her parents, who were still awake, started getting ready for bed in one of the interior rooms of the house.

Sandra fell from the second floor of her building on Calle Álvarez de Baena while watering the plants growing in the window box outside her balcony railing. She hit a tree before landing on the sidewalk, which slowed her descent. A young man studying in an apartment across the street heard a scream and a crash, went to the window, and, when he saw her body lying on the pavement, hurried downstairs.

TO THE HOSPITAL

Assisted by a taxi driver and a group of passersby, the student brought her to the urgent care at 1 de Montesa. From there, she was taken to the Residencia Sanitaria Francisco Franco.

TELLING HER PARENTS

Meanwhile, her father, hearing a commotion on the street, had gone down to the lobby and, through the glass front doors, saw a body on the ground. He hadn't brought his keys, though, so he had to go back upstairs. On descending once more and emerging from his building, Mr. Boris Mozarowsky heard the awful news and took off for the Hospital Universitario La Paz, where he assumed his daughter would be.

After he left, the taxi driver, the student, and another man arrived at the Mozarowsky home

```
to tell the family what had happened and where
Sandra had been taken. Someone tracked Mr. Mo-
zarowsky down at La Paz and let him know Sandra
was at Francisco Franco, and the whole family
came here [sic].
```

When something stretches credence, Brits say it "beggars belief," which this outlandish "reconstruction of events" certainly does. We can doubt that Sandra and her father were at the movies until 3:00 A.M. and that she'd decide to water plants in the middle of the night (and, for that matter, that her mom would be up watching *Esta noche fiesta*, directed by José María Íñigo, which I occasionally watched: it wasn't on that late), but these are minor details. What beggars belief is that she "leaned too far over the railing" to water her plants, which grew in planters on the balcony floor. She'd have watered them by crouching down, not by stretching her hand, arm, and half her body into space. If she'd done that, she'd have watered the street and left her plants dry.

"Sandra loved to go on her balcony," according to *Lecturas*' extensive coverage of her funeral, which is accompanied by images of the actress both sitting in a white chair on her balcony and leaning on its railing. When she's sitting, the railing is head-height; when she's standing, it's up to her chest. In order to plunge from the balcony, she'd have had to be standing on the chair.

Equally implausible is the idea that a young man studying across the street heard her scream and fall while her parents, awake in the very apartment she fell from, did not. Besides, why didn't her dog (she's cradling a lapdog in the photos for her "posthumous" *Primera Plana* interview) bark? It also beggars belief that, in the middle of the night in August 1977, a residential street in Madrid would have been so full of passersby. Families took long summer vacations back then, such that the wealthy neighborhoods of big cities were all but deserted in August. No one would have been there. And if the unnamed "student, taxi driver, and passersby" *were* there, why wouldn't they call the police and an ambulance as we've all been taught to do? Why would they assume the risk and responsibility of cramming a badly injured girl into a cab—she'd have been propped up between them, unconscious and drenched in blood—and taking her to a clinic themselves?

It beggars belief that her father, on hearing a "commotion," didn't go out on the balcony, to which the door was open and where his daughter no longer stood. Instead, he decided to go downstairs, where he saw a "body"—his daughter's body wrapped in her kimono—lying on the sidewalk outside their building, and failed to recognize her! It beggars belief that he went upstairs for his keys when he could easily have propped the door open and stuck his head out to see if the body was Sandra; that, on going up for his keys, he didn't notice that his daughter was gone; that his wife, who also knew she was awake and "watering the plants," also failed to notice her absence. It beggars belief that when Sandra's father came back down with his keys moments later, the body, the taxi driver, the student, and the passersby had all vanished. Luckily, other "passersby" (such a crowd on Álvarez de Baena at 3:00 in the morning!) were standing by to inform him that the victim was his own daughter (how did they know?). And, more than anything else, it beggars belief that Sandra's mother chose to wait comfortably at home rather than accompanying her husband to the hospital where, for all she knew, her daughter was dying. No mother would do that. Not the most soulless mother in the world. But in order to make this ridiculous story work, someone had to be at home on Álvarez de Baena to open the door for the "taxi driver, the student, and another man" when they showed up at dawn to tell her parents that Sandra was at Francisco Franco, not La Paz. Oh, and if she never regained consciousness and had no ID, how could they have known who she was or where to look for her family?

"Don't lies eventually lead to the truth? . . . Sometimes it is easier to see clearly into the liar than into the man who tells the truth. Truth, like light, blinds. Falsehood, on the contrary, is a beautiful twilight that enhances every object," Camus wrote in *The Fall*.

No one reported Sandra's fall to the police. No ambulance drove her, barefoot and nearly naked, through the early morning to the Residencia Hospitalaria Francisco Franco. No parent was with her when she was admitted, and neither of them showed up for hours, because when she had her "accident" they weren't around. All this is what the scrabbled-together official history is meant to conceal or to justify, but just calls attention to instead.

What really happened?

I don't know. All I have is what was written in the moment and what's been written all these years later. Her death was unexplained and mired in "mysterious circumstances," a phrase that appears over and over, demanding the conjecture, gossip, and rumors into which the case of Sandra Mozarowsky devolved.

Was it a fall? Was it a jump?

I've seen Sandra die onscreen over and over. I can conjure the fear in her eyes as she plunged downward in her kimono (not the white blouse!). I can hear her scream, that shriek I've listened to so many times. Her death could be a scene from one of her erotic horror movies. I suppose, though, that she would have had one expression if she jumped, another if she was pushed. If the former, it would've been set determination; if the latter, incredulity and fear.

It's a rumor, yes. It circulates online and appears in the occasional book, including the aforementioned *Ladies of Spain* by Andrew Morton, who writes, "Supposed royal lovers included, among others, the Italian singer Raffaella Carrà and the very young actress Sandra Mozarowsky, who died under mysterious circumstances. All we know for sure is that she fell from her balcony while watering plants; it appeared to be a suicide, but sinister whispers suggested that it was really the work of someone afraid she could put the Royal Family in a corner."

Critic Emilio de Gorgot includes a similar insinuation in a piece for the culture magazine *Jot Down* called, "Legends of '70s Erotic Cinema: Where'd They Go?," as does Marta Sanz in her novel *Daniela Astor y la caja negra*. Journalist Javier Bleda alludes directly to the potential murder in his biography of Mario Conde, writing in a discussion of yet another of the king's girlfriends, Bárbara Rey, that if "the statements the socialist politician Julián Sancristóbal made in prison were true, which I don't doubt for a moment given that his role gave him access to classified information, then we see that Bárbara (Rey) might very well have recorded herself as a means of protection from being suicided off a balcony (Sandra, we remember you)."

As for Rebeca Quintans's *Juan Carlos I: La biografía sin silencios*, it states that the "romance, if that's the word" Sandra had with the king was *vox populi*, and that "Sandra got pregnant. She discussed it with her people while making cryptic, unexpected public statements about going to live in London. She also maintained surreptitious contact with an Italian periodical in which no report about her ever appeared. She died unexpectedly in a fall from the balcony of her home on Calle del Barquillo in Madrid. An accident seemed implausible, and so people spoke for a while about suicide, though even her brother León Mozarowsky doubted that. It made no sense. But the case was never investigated in depth."

My guess is that Rebeca Quintans has been reading blogs about Sandra's death, given that she repeats their errors and lies. She echoes the blog *Espía en el congreso*, which incorrectly puts the accident on Calle del Barquillo, as well as another one, *Historias de mediocridad*, which, in its detailed exegesis of the story, gets the street right but has Sandra tumbling from the fourth floor, not the second, and mentions her supposed pregnancy. According to the latter blog, Jorge Rivero, "the Mexican actor and very close friend" of Sandra's, "may speak someday about the mysterious circumstances surround her death, the cover-up that followed it, and the secrets his dear Sandra told him." It also has her younger brother León Mozarowsky saying, "Her boyfriend—a real, ahem, king of the hill—dumped her for another famous girl. Sandra wanted to go public about it, tell the press everything. She even reached out to an Italian paper. She was getting insistent about it, and she wasn't even five months yet. One week short."

Sandra had no brother León. León or Lev Mozarowsky isn't real, or is real only in the internet's imagination. Sandra had two siblings, Alexis and Tatiana, both older than she was. When her mother, María del Rosario Ruiz de Frías, died, the obituary that ran in *ABC* on May 2nd, 2008, names her surviving children, Tatiana and Alexis, as well as her grandchildren, none of whom are called León or Lev.

Crónicas Borbónicas, a website that demanded "Justice for Sandra Mozarowsky," is no more, though others, like Foro del Atlético de Madrid, Burbuja Info: Foro de Economía, and the journalist Consuelo García Cid's blog, took up the mantle when it went offline. Every one of them refers to *Escrito en un libro*, a novel that the writer Pablo Blas first released under the name Tom Farrell with Editorial Séneca and then reissued himself without the pseudonym. In it, Blas digs right into the mysterious circumstances of Sandra's death, giving his character the name Sandra Wagneroski. His novel speculates that the secret police were involved in the actress's death, that they tried to intimidate her into shutting up and getting an abortion. He writes that two journalists from the ultra-right newspaper *El Alcázar* got a tip about a repentant heavyweight and investigated what had happened, but were censored before their conclusions got into print.

Was Sandra pregnant when she died? Her autopsy was never released to the public. In the photos for her posthumous interview in *Lectura*, which were shot a month before her "tragic fall," she's at home in Madrid, wearing a loose "multicolored Mexican dress" that hides her figure, but can't conceal what the interviewer, Luis Milla, calls the "few extra kilos" she's gained. You can tell she's heavier just from her face, anyway. It had changed.

Milla writes, very pleased with himself, that "Sandra told us on the phone, 'I don't want to talk to anyone. I have nothing to say. A photo shoot? No. Why? I just want to forget for a while. We can see later.' But eventually, she agreed to speak with us." He describes Sandra as "happy on the outside, but she gives the impression that something else is going on beneath the surface. She strikes us as nervous rather than calm. *Unsatisfied*, I'd say."

Sandra tells him that she just got back from Mexico, where she was shooting her most recent movie, *Ángel negro* (which was actually made in Colombia), and then vacationing in Acapulco.

"With your Mexican boyfriend Jorge?" the interviewer asks.

"No, Jorge and I are done. We decided to close a very lovely chapter of our lives. But I still had a wonderful time in his country."

When I interviewed an actress from the *Ángel negro* cast, she said Sandra couldn't possibly have had a fling with Jorge Rivero. He was accompanied to the shoot by a highly attached girlfriend who, the actress told me, "I could hear moaning all night from my bungalow. I'd tell Jorge, 'Give it a break, okay? We're all plenty jealous already.' So no, he never looked at Sandra. She was too young for him, anyway." Besides, Sandra had her faithful agent Rosa García guarding her the whole time she was in Colombia. So if she never dated Jorge Rivero, why did she give the reporter the impression that she had? Or did she? Did she say "Jorge and I," or did the journalist make it up?

"But if everything is reality, it's absurd to suppose that an undersecretary is more real than a dream," Borges said (or they say he said). All the narratives of Sandra's death are as tangled and confusing as a dream, and, for that matter, as useless as an undersecretary. In her interview with Luis Milla, she says (or they say she said) she's planning to go to London to "study English and drama." In her other posthumous interview, the one in *Primera Plana*, she says she's planning to "go to New York and do classes with Elia Kazan so I can learn to act while thinking in English." According to other outlets, she was preparing to shoot a new movie, or check into a weight-loss center in Marbella, or had already submitted herself to a strict regimen at a famous clinic there. Various tabloids and some real newspapers, including *ABC*, repeat the error of Sandra "tumbling from the fourth floor," not the second, and in pieces published both before and after her death, they harp on the perils of amphetamines, comparing Sandra to the drugs' most famous victims, Judy Garland and Marilyn Monroe.

One tabloid repeats Sandra's assertion that "abortion, to me, is a crime. It's acceptable if the mother is in serious danger, but we all understand that actions have consequences, and a human life isn't something to take lightly." Meanwhile, the quote *Primera Plana* used as the headline of their interview was, "Nobody knows I'm a virgin. They wouldn't understand." Was that random, or was there a concerted effort to squash rumors that she was pregnant? *Chi lo sa* . . . But I'm no detective, even if I'm playing one in these pages. I should go back to Wittgenstein, to whereof one cannot speak (even though our very rationality means enigmas fascinate us, challenge us, awaken our desire to understand, to understand ourselves through them, to light up the void of the unknown).

Sandra's alleged lover, the king, was on a state visit to Guatemala when she died. Her funeral, at the Instituto Anatomico-Forense on Calle Galileo, had rites performed by an Orthodox patriarch. In the photos, you can see her siblings, her maternal agent Rosa García, her grandmother, her father, her mother wearing dark glasses, everyone holding lit tapers, faces pale. Her mother couldn't bear to see her daughter interred at the cemetery in Pozuelo de Alarcón. At the gravesite, her father tried to open the casket to say a last goodbye, but was dissuaded. Rosa García opened it, though, to give Sandra her rosary and crucifix; she fainted before the burial was done and had to be helped away. I read that detail in one of the many magazines that covered the funeral, which was attended by many celebrities: colleagues of the deceased, including Bárbara Rey, with whom she shared her royal boyfriend. Nadiuska, Sandra's presumed successor in the king's favor, didn't feel strong enough to go to the funeral, but she did send a wreath.

* * *

> To each, death has a gaze.
> Death will come and will bear your eyes.
> It will be like quitting a vice,
> like seeing in the mirror
> a dead face resurfacing,
> like listening to a shut lip.
> Voiceless, we will go spiraling down.

Did Sandra die for love like Cesare Pavese, who wrote those

lines? Pavese, the poet who spent his life obsessed with suicide; who declared that no one ever lacks a good reason to kill themselves; who wrote, "Now it is no longer a choice between survival and deciding to take the plunge; but between taking the plunge alone—as I have always lived—or taking a victim with me so that the world will remember." Pavese didn't plunge, though. He poisoned himself in a hotel room. Before he died, he wrote in his diary, "All this is sickening. Not words. An act. I won't write any more." (In another entry, he decides, "The act—the act—must not be a revenge. It must be a calm, weary renunciation, a closing of accounts, a private, rhythmic deed. The last remark.")

But a girl who takes her own life to spite her lover isn't calmly, wearily renouncing anything. For her, suicide is the reverse: a desperate last attempt to get her boyfriend's attention. Young people kill themselves not out of a lack of vitality but an excess, and you could even say that what they want isn't to disappear forever, just to punish the loved ones they leave behind. Suicide as a game; suicide but just for a while. If you can imagine it, Wittgenstein said, then it's possible.

I imagine Sandra starring in the movie of my life, should I ever merit a biopic. She may be dead, but she's the only one who could play me. Let me tell you about the role.

CHAPTER 5

VICE AND RUIN

IN THE FIRST SCENE we see Sandra lying down in her white blouse, bound with leather cords to a cot in what appears to be a cell, or is, at the very least, a room austere enough to satisfy even Wittgenstein: it has a low ceiling, white walls, and one small, iron-barred window, furnished only with a Formica table bolted to the floor; a metal chair, also bolted down; and a built-in white wardrobe on the rear wall, beside the bathroom door—oh, and a nightstand holding a book and a box of earplugs. She's asleep, but in the next shot, a gray-habited nun looms over the girl like a buzzard, a vulture. Sandra opens her sea-green eyes. "Sister," she says, "can you untie me?"

We see the nun from the front now. She has the same features as Miss Colton, the treacherous teacher from *El colegio de la muerte*, and on them we read her pleasure as Sandra starts struggling against the leather restraints. One of Sandra's breasts—the left one—escapes from the white blouse's low neck, and the nun licks her lips. She lets her eyes nearly close before she begins undoing the straps, moving slowly and plainly enjoying herself. (I don't remember what material they tied me to the bed with, but I do remember having to yell and yell before a nun came to liberate me—a wrinkled, whiskery, sexless little nun who, I'm glad to say, never licked her lips at me. I doubt that I ever wore a white blouse. I slept in a T-shirt and underwear. Also, I wasn't eighteen. I was twenty years older. I wasn't beautiful and healthy like Sandra, either, but I accept that in the cinematic version of my life, I have to allow some creative license.)

Cut to Sandra in the bathroom, naked except for a towel. She just got out of the shower. She puts toothpaste on her right index finger and writes on the mirror, *MARÍA JOSÉ, YOUR HUSBAND IS CHEATING ON YOU.* (I never did that, but I wish it had occurred to me. María José, with whom I shared a bathroom and a wall, shouted at and insulted her absent husband all night. "Asshole, I *know* you're cheating, I *know* you're screwing someone, and I'm going to get you for it, you son of a bitch!" I despaired at her paranoia—not because she was suffering, but because I was tied to the bed and couldn't get up and tell her to pipe down.)

Aerial shot of the psychiatric hospital's cafeteria. A line of nuts (sorry, *patients*) snakes patiently up to a mean nun with overplucked eyebrows and an expression devoid of sympathy—Miss Wilkins from *El colegio de la muerte.* It could be a scene of parishioners lining up in the nave of a church to take communion, but from the nun they receive not the body of Christ but pills in a white plastic cup. When Sandra's turn comes, she lowers her head humbly and says, in a mouse's voice, "My medication, Sister."

Miss Wilkins looks her over disdainfully, contorting her thin lips into a death's-head grin, and the viewers fear—*I* fear—that she'll refuse the girl's request, but eventually she puts the white cup in Sandra's shaking hand. Sandra clutches it, examining its contents openly, avidly: are all the pills there? None are missing? She'd count them if it wouldn't make her seem mistrustful. She swallows them, chasing them with a gulp of water.

Outside the hospital is a pitiful little patio where patients slouch sorrowfully in plastic chairs, or stand and chat in small clusters, or wander alone, disoriented, talking to the flagstones or themselves or Lord only knows, you can't guess what's happening in an insane person's head. Sandra sits apart, absently smoking a cigarette. Her air of detachment suggests that she's roaming her memories, vanishing into the past . . . (I couldn't remember a thing: pills corrode memory as if they were sulfuric acid, deforming it, turning time into Wittgenstein's endless, continuous present, through which I passed in a permanent stupor, evincing about as much inner life as the potted geranium Sandra's ashing into onscreen, but in a movie, you need flashbacks to contextualize the protagonist's present: how did she get here? How could she have fallen this low?)

Flashbacks

NIGHT. INTERIOR: SMALL, STYLISHLY DECORATED APARTMENT (my apartment was genuinely tiny, but I imagine the movie expanding the square footage a bit). Sandra sits at an oak table in her white blouse, head bowed over a virgin sheet of paper. She begins writing, her hand jerky and nervous, and

I'm curious about what she has to say, but the camera's behind her and her hair tumbles messily over her shoulders and onto the table and paper, and I can't see a word. When she's done, she straightens up, and the camera finally shows us her desolate face. She's crying so hard I doubt she can see the balcony (or, rather, the miniscule terrace) in front of her through her waterfall of tears. She rises abruptly, but don't worry, she doesn't go out to the balcony, let alone start teetering over the railing. She opens a prescription bottle and dumps its contents impatiently onto the table, then starts counting, separating one, two, three, twenty-five. For a moment, she contemplates her pill mountain. Then, decision: she jams the round pills into her mouth hurriedly, grabbing as many as she can, as if afraid somebody's going to come take them away. Afterward, she does something inexplicable: rather than wait for the sleeping pills to kill her, which they certainly will, she . . . picks up the phone! She tells the person on the other end (we don't learn who it is; only she knows) that she just tried to commit suicide.

A frantic, wailing ambulance; an emergency room; a pumped stomach: all of that awaits Sandra, who regains consciousness in the antiseptic whiteness of a hospital room under the frightened, loving, focused gaze of Jorge Rivero, her Mexican *Ángel negro* co-star.

(It wasn't one ambulance, one emergency room, or one suicide note; it was seven ambulances, seven emergency rooms, seven heaps of twenty-five pills, and seven suicide notes in six months, though by the end I wasn't bothering to write them anymore.)

Sandra is, as usual, tied to a cot. Fat black leather straps cross her ankles and shoulders. Dressed in his profession's distinctive white coat, Dr. Kruger, the romantic lead from *El colegio de la muerte,* reassures her while injecting her with anesthesia. Once she's asleep, a pair of nurses—Misses Colton and Wilkins—also in white, get to work, clamping an evil-looking band around her forehead like a tiara and jamming what looks like a giant blue plastic teething ring in her mouth, which Miss Wilkins has to open. After the preparations are done, Dr. Kruger signals the nurses and presses a button on a black machine sprouting wires that lead to Sandra's body, which convulses violently with each shock. She jerks and writhes, twisting her sheets until her torso—electrodes; white blouse—is revealed. One breast gets loose, then the other, jostling together as she thrashes. It's a new subgenre for her: erotic electroconvulsive therapy.

A psychiatrist's consulting room. Sandra in front of the desk, Dr. Kruger behind. "Why am I so depressed?" she asks.

"I'm not sure you are," he replies.

Prolonged silence, then a tense conversation in which Sandra, wounded, tells the psychiatrist he shouldn't question her illness. She's not a new patient. New to *him,* yes, but he's her seventh shrink. His predecessors all failed to treat her severe depression, but not one had trouble diagnosing it or deciding to attack it with pills, which are what Sandra wants from the good Dr. Kruger: a miracle prescription, antidepressants that will cure her instantly, maybe offer a fun little bonus high, some warm glittery feelings without a comedown. Oh, and speaking of *down,* she wants tranquilizers. Sleeping pills, too. She can't handle nights without the latter or days without the former; she needs them; it's the reason she made this appointment. Why else?

Dr. Kruger resists. He suggests that all these pills are, perhaps, the cause of Sandra's suffering. Not only does he refuse to prescribe them, but he also asks if she's high: he calls her an addict! Sandra! She's refused countless chances to try heroin; she's maintained a cautious, prudent relationship with recreational drugs (nothing but weed unless it's the weekend) for twenty years; she only takes antidepressants and tranquilizers under strict medical supervision. How could she be a drug addict? She feels insulted, abandoned, misunderstood. She *trusted* this man. On leaving his practice, she heads straight to a bar where she gets a water and, with wobbling hands, taps two tranquilizers out of the bottle in her purse. She's very anxious. She's got to calm down. (When Rosa Sender, my psychiatrist and friend, said I had to quit, I was equally outraged, indignant, frantic for my pills. I couldn't get clean. I could only bear life with drugs—and I wasn't bearing it, really, just sustaining a tricky, precarious equilibrium from one suicide attempt to the next. My life was a high-wire act, and not falling depended on getting the right balance of drugs and pills.)

Not long after her admission to the psych ward (con: getting tied to the bed; pro: all the pills a girl could want), Sandra goes for a walk near the clinic with her faithful, loving boyfriend, Jorge Rivero, his hand gently gripping her elbow. Jorge jokes with her, makes conversation, tries to distract her, but Sandra is stubbornly angry. She accuses him of imprisoning her, of just wanting to get rid of her, and then, abruptly, she wrenches herself free from his hand and sprints away. Walking, she moved so shakily you'd never imagine she could run, but Sandra's got *legs*. She's got wings. She flies ahead of the camera, ahead of her athletic boyfriend, who, implausible though this seems (and is), can't catch her. She's turning a corner, running down an avenue, disoriented, with no destination, just getting away from the hospital, leaving it in her dust—until two massive orderlies loom before her, grab her arms, and frog-march her inside, ignoring her kicking legs, her protests, her screams.

Now she's in the clinic's director's office, awaiting her reprimand. Dr. Kruger says that if she tries again—this flight was her third—he'll resort to drastic measures. He'll certify her incompetent. He's discussed it with her parents already.

Sandra is aware of the threat's gravity. Not in vain did she give so many years to the dignified practice of the law. She presents her case to Dr. Kruger—my *parents* are insane, not me; you should get them in here and set me free—sure he'll react to her story as sympathetically as all the psychiatrists she's seen (or seen through) before. She got them on her side by describing her awful childhood, her terrible parents, but she can't move Kruger, can't woo him. He's tough.

Sandra meditates on Dr. Kruger's insensitivity until a nun informs her that her boyfriend's visiting. Jorge Rivero joins her in the garden, smiling warmly, carrying a shopping bag stuffed with Tupperware. Sandra hates institutional food, and so Jorge brings her homemade meals, which she hardly touches. Depression's no good for the appetite.

"Baby," she says. She starts smiling, then catches herself: a true smile wouldn't be dignified in her condition. "I made a decision. I'm moving to Mexico after I get out. I'm ready for a fresh start."

MEXICO CITY. EXTERIOR: XOCHIMILCO CANAL. Mariachis sing, "Éstas son las mañanitas / que cantaba el rey David. / Hoy por ser día de tu santo / te las cantamos a ti." Floating on the trajinera *Carmelita,* shaded by a canopy painted in psychedelically bright colors—chartreuse, canary yellow, fuchsia, tangerine—sitting at a table dense with bouquets, Sandra sips tequila and beer and snacks on tamales and tiny sandwiches (she drinks more than she eats; really, she hardly eats at all). She's got pleasant company: the mariachis with their charro suits and cheery singing, their violins and guitars; her *chevalier servant,* Jorge Rivero; and a chatty, affectionate group of his Mexican friends singing him "Las Mañanitas," since it's his birthday.

Sandra seems happy. She's snuggling with her boyfriend; her eyes shine; she's smiling; she's got a bright red flower in her hair. Has a miracle come to pass? Did Mexico cure her depression? Or is she just singing and clapping and living it up because she's drunk?

MEXICO CITY. INTERIOR: HOTEL ROOM (A *NICE* HOTEL, LUXURIOUS, I HAD MONEY IN THOSE DAYS). Sandra lounges in a king bed while Jorge crouches by the far wall, digging through a suitcase. He looks confused, surprised.

"I thought I told you not to bring drugs to Mexico."

"And I didn't!" Sandra says immediately. "No weed, no hash, no coke."

"Just a hundred bottles of downers?"

"You said *drugs,* not medicine. I *need* those. It's not like I take them for fun."

INTERIOR: HOTEL BAR. Sandra and Jorge sit opposite each other at a high-top, holding hands. Jorge's watching her. She's got that familiar glaze, that distant, troubled, hopeless expression that tells us she's not seeing him at all.

"Would you like to go to the Museum of Anthropology?" he suggests gently.

"No. I'm depressed. I'd like a margarita."

EXTERIOR: MEXICO CITY. NIGHT. PLAZA GARIBALDI. SIX MARGARITAS LATER. Crowds jam the square, singing and dancing to the rancheras, salsas, and cumbias that colorfully dressed groups of mariachis play. It's a joyful scene, celebratory, overflowing with extras and outrageously pricey to shoot. Sandra is in a cantina beneath an arcade, mariachis serenading her. She's changed into the "multicolored Mexican dress" from her posthumous *Lectura* photo shoot, and in it, she dances barefoot on the table, dodging plates, ashtrays, tequilas, beers, bowls, glasses. "Con dinero y sin dinero / hago siempre lo que quiero / y mi palabra es la ley. No tengo trono ni reina, ni nadie que me comprenda / pero sigo siendo el reeeey!," she belts. She'll be as hoarse as a mariachi by the end of the night, but her balance, rhythm, and grace on that table would do her ballet teachers proud. (I, meanwhile, was probably a pathetic sight up there, surrounded by mariachis, drunkenly kicking bottles and spilling drinks and scattering cigarette ash everywhere.)

VOICEOVER: *Valle de Bravo, southeast of Mexico City, is the hottest weekend getaway for residents of both Toluco and the capital. Situated beside an enormous manmade lake, this town of adobe walls, red roofs, and cobbled streets offers not only a wide selection of hotels, artisan goods, golf, and dining, but also* *exciting aquatic recreation and extreme sports such as paragliding and hang gliding.* (Yes, voiceovers are irritating, but this production wouldn't have happened without great effort and generous grants, and we're showing our gratitude with a little travel information. It's really the least we could do.) *Before there was a lake, when this town was called San Francisco del Valle de Tenascaltepec, a tremendous forest grew facing the mountains. Now there's a Valle de Bravo for all ages, all tastes, all budgets: boutiques and open markets, delicatessens and delights*, and Sandra and Jorge Rivero, strolling hand in hand on the cobblestones like tourists, though Sandra's not one, she'd rather not be, she's going to live here, rent a casita and restart her life in *an Eden of endless surprises—except the weather, which is good year-round—of forest vistas; of monarch butterflies, who winter right here.*

Sandra couldn't give less of a shit about butterflies. She's not wasting her time on hikes with a net. She came to write. Write *what*? She's not sure yet, but it'll come. She tells Jorge that, anyway, to reassure him. He's the jittery one now, tense and tortured about leaving her for Barcelona, his obligations, his life. It's a sad goodbye scene, moving, though I thought the violin soundtrack wasn't necessary: Sandra's beautiful, teary eyes and Jorge's sorrowful body language were plenty. She'll miss him, he'll miss her, and yet she's resolved. She's going to live and write in Valle de Bravo. She's already rented her casita, complete with garden and pool, and the minute the landlord's got it ready, she's moving in. (Recently, while digging through a box I'd long forgotten, I found some photos of the house with its pool and garden. I had a two-story house! I had a pool and a garden! If only for three weeks.)

INTERIOR: HOUSE IN VALLE DE BRAVO. NIGHT. Sandra sleeps in a loft—a *tapanco,* it's called here—in a mountain house that her friend Victoria Vera's boyfriend has loaned her until her casita is ready. She's alone. Victoria's boyfriend is in the capital, and Victoria's out of the country. Since Sandra got to Mexico, she's heard countless tales of kidnappings and robberies, and tonight she's conquered the resulting fear with beer, tequila, double her usual dose of sleeping pills, and a joint laced with hypnotically effective hash oil. Her goal: a sleep so profound that if thieves break in, she won't hear them. If someone comes to rob, let them rob.

A man's weight on her body rouses her in the early morning. It's dark in the loft. She can't see, but she recognizes his voice. Sandra cries out, shouts, "No!," but the man, X, gags her with his hand and pins her with his weight. She stops struggling. She's not strong enough. She sinks into her drugged lethargy. After he's done, X switches a light on, and Sandra registers that he's as high as she is. Upsetting him isn't in her interest. X suggests a tequila and she says yes, wanting to get drunker or higher to mute the horror of what just happened, to scramble it, dull her sensitivity. She can hardly get down the wooden staircase, but once she's made it to the ground floor, she trails him into the living room, where he pours tequila and rolls a joint (and cuts her a line, but she demurs: it would ruin the pills' blurring effect). She sips her drink and smokes her weed, and next time she returns to consciousness, she's in the loft. X is a hefty guy, and after she passed out, he just slung her over his shoulder and carried her up the narrow staircase. Now he's moving on top of her again. What does Sandra feel? Fatigue. Disbelief. Emptiness.

Scenes from a Montage, Not Necessarily in Order

Sandra at her desk in her freshly painted house, either writing or pretending to. She can't concentrate, loses her resolve, and goes to the kitchen to mix a margarita, which she drinks in the garden, lounging in a hammock and studying her pool melancholically (soundtrack: Chavela Vargas).

Sandra by herself in a cantina with a margarita (hers are terrible). All the other patrons are male. All of them glance at her out of the corners of their eyes. Some seem curious, some reproachful.

Sandra in another cantina at daybreak with a michelada, chatting amicably with the other drinkers. Without warning, a man pulls a gun and sets it on the bar. As if a puppeteer had pulled a string, every other man does, too. (Maybe not *every* other man, maybe it was just two or three, but in my memory, that's how it happened: six pistols on the bar, the cantina's patrons happily discussing caliber and performance. Not me. I didn't speak; I had no idea what to say about guns. But I drank doggedly, smiling, pretending I was comfortable, pretending that I belonged.

Sandra returns home. Victoria Vera is waiting. Sandra says hello. Victoria Vera slaps her.

Sandra has a surprise visitor: Jorge Rivero! His arrival seems not to startle her. Maybe she anticipated that he couldn't go more than two weeks without her; maybe she's living in such chronic stupefaction, such numbness, that she can't feel surprise. At night, she throws her first and last Mexican party, which ends with all the guests swimming at sunrise. And a day later, she's gone. We don't hear Jorge persuade her, don't watch him pack her bags or buy their tickets to Barcelona. Her Mexican sojourn just ends.

My Mexican sojourn wrapped up similarly, though it wasn't a selfless partner who retrieved me, it was my brother Pablo. He left his life to save mine after my friend M. (Victoria Vera) begged him to, my friend who gave me the slap I was begging for as I careened into my house, my good friend M. who got sick of being my babysitter and rescuer during my calamitous time in Valle de Bravo. "I can't do it any longer," she said to Pablo. "Come get her."

M. summoned Pablo after getting an anguished call from my mother, who I'd just told for the hundredth time, if now from unusually far away, that I'd swallowed another fistful of pills. It was my mother and her sister Carmen who joined me on that idiotic trip to Mexico, not a beautiful man with movie-star teeth. It was my mother and Aunt Carmen on the trajinera in the Xochimilco canal, drinking margaritas in the hotel bar, dancing rancheras in Plaza Garibaldi, and it was them, my mother and Aunt Carmen, house-hunting with me in Valle de Bravo, and after they left, after my mom flew back to her husband and the rest of her children in Barcelona, I was sad. I missed her. I hadn't thought I could miss my mother, who I'd always fled. Now I wanted her by my side.

When I fell, like Lucifer, and got trapped in a cycle of overdose-recovery-relapse, our relationship transformed. A "normal" mom, the Hollywood American mom of my long-ago daydreams, wouldn't have tolerated a fraction of what my mother endured. It was she who sat up all night, waiting while I had my stomach pumped (I must've had the emptiest stomach in Spain); it was her face I saw on waking in the hospital, arms bristling with tubes and needles; and it was she who came daily to the psychiatric ward with meals I didn't eat, took me for walks I tried to escape from, she who got her period back out of nowhere, had cardiac arrhythmias, started losing her hair, couldn't sleep, suffered and suffered and yet, when anyone with an ounce of sense said, "When Clara calls you to say she swallowed another bottle of pills, don't call 112. Don't go to the ER. Let her die," my mother refused.

"Clara's my daughter," she said. "If she calls, if I know she's in danger, I'm going. I'm not giving up. She's my *daughter*."

I have an ounce of sense now. I have the authority of nineteen years of sobriety; I am, if not a pillar of society, perhaps a little stone in its wall; and now I'm the one talking to my mom, telling her, "Don't answer the phone. Cut her off. Let her die. She's going to kill you if things go on like this," but my mother refuses to listen.

Next I go to my father, since men, supposedly, are colder, more rational. I say, "Clara isn't worth it. She'd be better off dead. She's too pathetic to live and too cowardly to die. She's got no dignity. Her game of taking pills and calling you—she's putting *you* in charge of whether she kills herself. It's perverse and it's cruel."

But he won't listen, either. "If she calls," he says, "I'll go. No matter what. I'll always try to save my girl."

"Can't you tell she's just going to do it again?" I snap. "She's incurable."

INTERIOR: BARCELONA: HOME. Sandra, just back from Mexico, sits at a table. (Again? Again.) It's round this time, and upholstered in worn green felt. On it are a full glass of water and an array of pills; to vary the repeated scene, this time the glass is tall and beveled and the pills are a different color and size. Sandra regards the black television screen in front of her (it's not on; she's just looking at it because it's there) with an expression that's difficult to parse. Using only her eyes, her lowered eyebrows, and her creased forehead, she's attempting to convey a mixture of profound doubt, uncertainty, misgiving, and fear, with a hint of wild hope mixed in. Our director's asking a lot from her here, and besides, what her suffering eyes *should* tell us is that she's desperate, for reasons we don't know: not even I can remember the reason for my misery. But like Maria, the young Italian girl who died by suicide in the train tunnel, she's arrived at the certainty that she's no one in this world. She has no possibilities. Her life isn't worth living, and she refuses to trudge up the mountain with her rock one more time. (She's not immortal like Sisyphus: she can cut her sentence short.) Once she starts entertaining the notion of death, she surprises herself with her intense curiosity. Like Virginia Woolf, she has the sense that dying will be a great excitement—something positive, active. She suspects that a pleasant surprise will await her. Didn't Wittgenstein say that only death gives life its meaning? When she dies, then, she'll understand it all.

Or maybe she'll understand nothing. It doesn't matter. She's too busy with her excitement, the vertigo of standing at the precipice, which alarms her: she's afraid, she's warning herself, she's asking, Well, are we dying or not? What did we decide? She wants to kill herself, but just for a while.

(Disembodied voices start joining this silent scene.)

"You should only poison yourself when you truly want to poison yourself," says Wittgenstein.

"Not words. An act. Don't write any more!" orders Pavese.

"You can drown yourself in the river," murmurs Woolf.

"Jump!" she tells herself.

I spent two days in a coma at the Clínica Teknon in Barcelona (or, rather, my mother spent them, shaking as she guarded my body in the ICU. My memory of that time, like the others, is gone). Although it failed to kill me, my last overdose successfully damaged my vital organs: my heart, my lungs, my kidneys, my liver, and my brain, my goddamn brain, whose responsibility all this was.

Rosa Sender came to visit. She was commendably patient: she, too, refused to give up on me, but this time, she was furious. "You're not going to kill yourself," she said, "but if you do this again, you're going to wake up paraplegic."

I was shaken. Death was a risk I could run; disability was not. It was the first time my game frightened me.

"Why are you doing this?" she asked. "Why do you keep doing this?"

I couldn't answer. I had no why. It was a compulsion. It was inexplicable, and yet I tried to defend myself, to justify myself, by saying, "I'm not. It isn't *me*. I'm a different person."

But Rosa was looking at my face, hearing my voice, seeing my body. I could sense her skepticism. How could this not be me?

INTERIOR: BATHROOM. Sandra faces the mirror. Before her is the mutilated countenance of the mad scientist from *El colegio de la muerte*. She hides behind her hands, horrified. When she peeks, we catch glimpses of a bridgeless nose, a lidless eye, scarred skin, and what was once a sexy Slavic pout but is now a mean, thin-lipped rictus. She retreats, leaves the bathroom, takes a breath, and confronts the mirror anew. In it is the grotesque mad scientist. She recoils, calms herself, tries again—and again she sees an atrocity: mangled flesh, withered lips, no nose or eyebrows or lashes or lids. So this is her. It's how she sees herself, anyway. What do others see? She needs to know.

But we're getting ahead of ourselves. We fast-forwarded some crucial scenes: Sandra's mother (Mónica Randall) driving her to a resort, a pretty, semicircular three-story building, sixties-looking, with a gorgeous garden, an elaborate mini-golf course, and a pool set in its verdant lawn, surrounded by waiting lounge chairs. A nurse (Miss Colton, naturally, in a short-sleeved white jacket, white pants, and dark clogs) meets Sandra at reception. After Sandra says goodbye to her mother, the nurse leads her to her room, which is sunny, with a view of the garden. Sandra would like to push aside the curtains and open the windows, but she's distracted by the nurse, who, bizarrely, has started to ransack her luggage, tossing its contents unceremoniously on the carpet, digging through her clothes like a customs inspector. Next she grabs Sandra's purse without asking—Sandra is speechless with indignation anyway—and dumps it out on the bed, then rifles through her toiletries, which yields results: triumphantly, she snatches Sandra's perfume and nail clippers.

"You can have them back when you go," she promises. She informs Sandra she has to remain in her room until given permission to leave, then hands her some pills (which Sandra plainly wasn't expecting) and waits for her to take them. She spots and confiscates Sandra's laptop, then, on her way out, rolls her eyes at the heap of novels she removed from

Sandra's bags. "What'd you pack those for?" she says. "We've got our books here."

Where is Sandra?

What's wrong with this resort? Who treats guests like this?

In the next scene, the mystery is revealed. A nurse (Miss Colton, of course) liberates Sandra from her solitude and escorts her to a big room with tall windows and rows of individual desks, like a classroom. She hasn't had any human contact since arriving at the resort, but now she's surrounded by men and women chatting amongst themselves, though their conversations all paused when Sandra walked in.

A woman breaks the ice. "You're the new girl, right? Did you just get off Devil's Island? Why are you here? Drinking? Cocaine? Pills, like me?"

Sandra's in rehab. Devil's Island is the patients' name for the isolation the clinic imposes on anyone taking detox medication, which has side effects that include vertigo and fainting. (Sandra napped contentedly through her time on Devil's Island. She hadn't gotten that much sleep in ages.) Now she's embarking on group therapy, led by Jorge Rivero (we've got the cast we've got), an addict turned counselor. He pressures her to admit to her fellow patients that, yes, why lie, she's abused drugs for a while, but the ones that plunged her into hellish chaos, the ones that got her here, are tranquilizers and sleeping pills.

"You have a polysubstance use disorder," Jorge Rivero tells her (which, in Sandra's opinion, is an exaggeration). "Your drug of choice is benzodiazepine." *Drug of choice* sounds fun, lucky, pleasurable. Here, though, it means *the drug that almost killed you.*

As the session goes on, the addicts raise their hands and wait their turns to speak. Each contribution is a confession. (Ludwig would have thrived here.) One man recalls robbing banks at gunpoint (with his "piece," he says, adding that he's still not used to life without it) before admitting that he was "powerless over his addiction" (more rehab language) to cocaine, which he has now sworn to live without. Another man describes lying to his wife, claiming he was going on a work trip, when in fact he went no further than his building's garage, where he holed up in his car with a stash of cocaine for three days. A small-town housewife says through gritted teeth that she hid wine bottles in closets and plant pots. A young man took his one-year-old daughter from her crib while her mother slept, put her in the car, got on the highway, and, with his baby in her seat in the back, did lines in a vacant lot until sunrise. Her company soothed him, he explains; it brought him peace.

Sandra listens to these tales as if she were an anthropologist. She's politely interested, surprised, horrified, moved. After therapy, she joins the addicts at a long table in a private section of the hotel dining room, separated by a discreet arch from the tables where the resort's other guests, primarily pensioners on vacation, watch them with a mix of curiosity and suspicion that, when the groups mix, will give way to sympathy. At the pool, a retiree from Huelva will ask Sandra, "What are you? Cocaine or alcohol?," and she'll shake her wet hair back and say happily, "Pills," then dive into the water again.

Sandra swims five hundred meters every day before breakfast. She likes the pool. She likes the garden, the morning hikes in the nearby forest, the resort food, the tan she's getting, she has to admit she likes the mini-golf course, she likes it all, but she hates therapy. It offends her. She hasn't spoken since her introduction to the group. She makes no effort to hide her disinterest and enervation, and Jorge Rivero scolds her for her silence, her apathy, her refusal to start the work.

One day, Sandra raises her hand. An expectant murmur runs through the room. On rising, she glowers around her and says, "*You're* addicts. *I'm* insane."

That was what I said to Rosa Sender and to my parents during the long phone calls I made when my companions were in therapy. I was in the wrong place. I wasn't an addict, just a sensitive, tortured soul who required sympathy, support, and freedom, yes, freedom, which I was denied: though I was no longer on Devil's Island, I couldn't leave the resort until eleven days after my arrival, and then only chaperoned by a long-time inmate. Besides, the guards—the medical and psychiatric teams—demanded not just that I quit my pills (no problem: my tolerance was so high I was immune), but that I abstain from alcohol and all other intoxicants until I died. I considered a sober life not worth living, though I had the wisdom to keep that opinion to myself. Instead I announced to the head doctor that I was quitting treatment. My family braced for the worst: my return. I got my perfume, nail clippers, and laptop back, I packed my bags—and then I called my mom to tell her not to come get me. I wasn't leaving yet. My troubles with pills had started with insomnia, and in rehab, after I was through with the detox medication, I slept poorly; as I prepared to leave, it hit me that I couldn't confront my sleeplessness alone. I'd start taking sleeping pills again, it wouldn't help, and soon I'd be seething through the nights, deranged by insomnia, which would restart the cycle: the mountain of pills, the heavy return to consciousness in the hospital, the psych ward, the restraints, the whiskery nun ignoring my cries.

So I didn't go. I stopped misbehaving. I spent nearly three months in rehab, participating actively in therapy, confessing my sins, swearing to all the gods on Olympus that I accepted my powerlessness over my addiction and wouldn't touch drugs again. I sat through their film screenings and put real effort into the questionnaires we had to do afterward, though it was the wrong effort: I critiqued the rehab movies' stupidity, their simple, didactic plots, their terrible scripts and stiff performances and clumsy cinematography. At some point Dr. Kruger (I may as well call him that) clarified the assignment and I changed my ways, writing dutifully that I'd gotten the message, which was that drugs are bad. My docility's only limit was that I never read their preferred book, *Me llamo Ramón y soy drogadicto*. A nurse tried to get me to discuss it, but I told her I'd heard Ramón had relapsed and was afraid it could harm my recovery to read his memoir.

One winter day they let me go.

I should have been happy. Instead, I was scared. I was afraid of myself (like Wittgenstein, my hell is myself) and my new purity, my future without drinking, smoking, cocaine, or pills. How was I supposed to sleep? In rehab, my system was compliance. I followed the rules. I woke early, swam, ate breakfast, hiked with the other patients, had therapy, sat through the daily screening, more therapy, communal dinner. If I did all that, I slept, and I only cared about sleeping. At home, from the instant I rose to the cursed moment I got back in bed, my every thought and deed was aimed at courting slumber. Soon I found that my black chamois trousers gave me insomnia. My jeans, in contrast, promoted sleep, so I wore them until they grew so intolerably filthy I had to wash them, which destroyed their soporific effect. I said a sorrowful goodbye to my suede ankle boots (brutal insomnia) and an angry one to my black coat (never should've put it on). My diet was also relevant: chard gave me three straight nights of acceptable sleep, though Night 4 went wrong (maybe it was too heavily sautéed), while tomatoes, veggie fried rice, and albóndigas con sepia meant sleeplessness and misery.

I tried so hard to learn the rules. I gave it my all. But the game kept changing. Since no food was consistently safe, I quit eating, growing as emaciated as I was in my adolescent anorexic stage. Speaking to my fellow patients when I went to group therapy gave me insomnia. Speaking to my parents and siblings gave me insomnia. Using white trash bags gave me insomnia; reading the paper gave me insomnia; greeting the doorman when I went out gave me insomnia—and then one day I looked in the mirror and wasn't there.

I'd transformed.

In the mirror I saw my face, but distorted: off-center nose, mean mouth, overplucked eyebrows, and eyes—the eyes belonged to a lunatic. I asked my parents if I looked different to them; I asked my siblings, my fellow patients, whether they'd noticed the change, and all of them said, "What are you talking about? Your face is the same as it's always been." I knew they were lying, though. I could hear it in their voices, and I could see it in their lowered eyes.

I was ashamed to wear my new face out in public. When I took the train to the resort for therapy, I struggled not to tell the other passengers that this wasn't my real face: I had another, better one, which I'd be getting back any day. Every morning I hurried to the mirror, and every morning that horrifying new face, mine but not mine, lay in wait. It was at that point that I moved back into my parents' house, into my childhood room, since I couldn't take care of myself and my mother was tortured by the thought that she shouldn't have taken me to rehab, that rehab had made me even worse. In the early mornings when I wandered barefoot out of my room, having given up on falling asleep, I found her waiting at her desk in the study with a cigarette and a book, having spent the night in an unhappy vigil, even though she had no idea how to help me when I inevitably arose. My father didn't know either, and neither did my siblings. My family had come to the sad conclusion that I was a lost cause. I would never regain my sanity. I was going to spend my life as a silent, malevolent leech, unable to hold a conversation or even read a newspaper, prisoner of the monomaniacal thought that I'd gotten into the shower with my left foot, not my right, I was a moron, I'd guaranteed that I wasn't going to sleep, the only way I could possibly counteract the insomniac effect of my morning slip-up was to put my right foot ahead of my left for the rest of the day, there was no room for error, and so I couldn't let myself get distracted by talking to anyone even if they spoke to me, I had to concentrate—but my mother tried so relentlessly to get my attention that I always caved, and, in caving, turned to her with my left foot first.

Ignore what the literature professors say about madness. It's terrifying to be insane.

Sandra's back at the resort. She hasn't relapsed, which raises the other patients' hackles. "What's she doing here?" they ask. On seeing her state, though, they realize she's been committed again because she's out of her mind. Some of them protest, demand that she be transferred to a psychiatric hospital, since all she's going to do here in rehab is irritate everyone. If she could speak, if she weren't trapped in her manias, she would defend herself. I'm not insane, she'd say. I'm an addict!

In therapy, Jorge Rivero shows her to new arrivals. "If you don't quit," he says, "you'll end up like her." Sandra's hurt, naturally, but she's proud, too. No one's ever held her up as an example before. She begins cherishing a secret hope that her presence is useful, that she could be their model of the ravages of drug use and, in that capacity, get to live here permanently. With a couple exceptions, the other patients are kind to her. She follows like a dog when groups go to town; alone, she wouldn't be able to cross the street. She can't chat, can't argue, can't get a word out—she, who once had so many words—but at one of the little sober goodbye parties for a departing patient, she sneaks unexpectedly into a group photo. She wants to see whether the camera captures the old face or the new.

She goes forty-eight hours without sleeping. She smells of sweat and fear (fear has an odor: it stinks of corralled animals). She feels a weight in her head, hears a constant murmur. Inside her skull is an overheated motor on the verge of stalling, and she needs to get it out, get the weight out, get the sound out, get out the single thought that bangs bangs bangs at her mind like a fly looking for the way out of a fly bottle—and then she remembers that *she* has a way out.

I'd read *Anna Karenina* three times, but she didn't cross my mind. (Later I kicked myself for that failure, which tells you what a pedant I am.) La Garriga, the town near Barcelona where the Blancafort resort is located, has a train station. A train could free me. It could do for me what it did for poor Italian Maria, or for glamorous, tragic Anna Karenina: it could liberate me from the head that had turned into my enemy.

Clara Usón

Split Screen

LEFT: Dr. Sender (Victoria Vera) tries to persuade Dr. Kruger that Sandra's having a major obsessive-compulsive episode; that she's only going to get worse until she starts ECT. Dr. Kruger, smiling slightly, dismisses her with an arrogant wave and a shake of his head.

RIGHT: Sandra sprints as if running for her life. She gets out of the resort and heads to the station, but before she can carry out her terrible mission, a squadron of other patients who have guessed her intention catch her.

LEFT: Dr. Sender is mute. Dr. Kruger, in the center of the screen, listens as a nurse tells him what Sandra has done. He furrows his brow and lifts his right eyebrow, then his left (nobody's furrowed a brow or lifted an eyebrow in this novel yet: it's about time). He reaches for the intercom and gives orders dispassionately.

I started getting shots of Anafranil for OCD that day. When the nurses came to administer it in the mornings, I always asked how long until I got my old face back, and one day it returned. I looked in the mirror and there I was. I was me again. (If, that is, I'm anyone. "I" is only a pronoun, as Ludwig would say, and pronouns, like all other words, are unfaithful. Turn your back, and they change what they mean.)

After I was discharged, I moved in with my parents again, and my mother and father made a change to their lives that would have struck them as complete nonsense if they hadn't been doing it for me: they quit drinking at home. It was the only way the doctor would let me live with them. A year later, I was still there, still fumbling back toward sanity (if I'm sane, that is: my family still has their doubts). My life was gym in the morning, therapy in the afternoon. My psychologist was helping me regain the ability to choose. I'm talking about tiny, semiconscious decisions: what to order at a restaurant, whether to wear a yellow sweater or a gray argyle one. Negligible little choices like that gave me horrible, debilitating anxiety. Fernando Gutiérrez, the psychologist, coached me to leave them up to luck: heads bus, tails metro, and if I slept poorly, so be it. Sometimes I cheated, though, and then called him, contrite and ashamed, to confess.

My medical team wouldn't let me return to my legal work until I was fully recovered. No one said I couldn't write fiction, though. According to my mother, writing novels is a hobby like needlepoint or golf, and hobbies are inherently harmless. Besides, who besides myself could I harm if a novel went wrong? (Danilo Kiš, the Serbian novelist, said that writing is for people with nothing left to lose; writing is an expression of hopelessness. According to Kiš, the choice is between the typewriter and the noose. I'm shy, but I'm a worthless assassin. I can't hang myself, I've got nothing to lose, and so I write.)

Our movie has a new title. We are now watching

VICE AND REDEMPTION

Sandra is in a tent at a festival, signing copies of her novel *El colegio de la muerte* for thousands of readers who have waited for hours in line in the hot sun to meet her, their favorite author. *El colegio de la muerte* has been translated into three hundred languages and sold thirty million copies worldwide. A book that successful is, surely, a masterpiece.

In a solemn yet moving ceremony, the Minister of Health awards Sandra the Medal of the Good Addict. Her boyfriend, her doctor, and her parents (Jorge Rivero, Victoria Vera, Mónica Randall, and Carlos Ballesteros) applaud furiously.

Wedding bells ring! Sandra and Jorge are married—

* * *

. . . but no, I can't let this go on. We're taking too many liberties; I liked the old title better; you can't end an erotic horror movie with a wedding; and mine isn't a story of overcoming, just surviving. If I could, I'd tell Sandra, citing Borges, that suffering has no merit and no moral. It's not a teacher, and life isn't school.

From that part of my life, I have retained a deep-seated fear of drugs and insanity, as well as a sensation of liberty. It seems to me that I should really be dead, and that each year I keep living is a gift to be used in any way I like. I no longer feel obligated to justify my existence or devote myself to serious, worthwhile work. Having been insane means I no longer have social responsibilities (or that's what I've decided, irresponsibly). My novels are the rocks I push up the mountain, and when each one is done I see that it hasn't met my expectations, that I fucked up, and that I have no choice but to start from the bottom again.

Pavese wrote in his diary, "Literature is a defense against

the attacks of life. It says to life: 'You can't deceive me. I know your habits, foresee and enjoy watching your reactions, and steal your secret by involving you in cunning obstructions that halt your normal flow.'" I relate. My novels are worlds of shadows that I create to defend myself from the attacks of life. I feel comfortable in them, since I'm only a shadow myself.

Three months before my mother died, while we were setting the table in her dining room, she described her funeral to me in detail. She wanted a "simple," secular ceremony and a restrained obituary without any clichés about her "grieving husband." She'd rather be cremated than buried, and she wanted the ashes "out with the trash. None of that foolishness about taking them up a mountain or renting a boat to release them at sea." She was always a practical, unsentimental woman.

I was uncomfortable during the conversation. I tried making jokes, but she ignored them and kept giving me her instructions. Later I learned that she'd been talking to her friends about dying for a while. She was calm about it, almost indifferent, treating it as imminent but not sad or unpleasant. My mother wasn't sick, though, and she was only seventy years old. She'd had bypass surgery—thank you, smoking and alcoholism—and her general practitioner had told her that if she didn't take better care of herself she'd end up in a wheelchair. It was a terrifying prospect: she was highly autonomous, accustomed to doing everything for herself and everyone else. She couldn't bear the thought of dependence.

After the surgery, we, her family, devoted ourselves to the impossible task of getting her to stop drinking and smoking and live healthily. She snuck cigarettes, like I had as a teenager, and hid wine in closets and behind rows of books on shelves.

We badgered her into going to therapy, and years later, the psychologist told me that my mother had struck her as a lonely, lost, disoriented woman. I protested: I said that she had her family around her, though the truth was that my dad was usually at work, and my siblings and I had moved out and learned to take care of ourselves long before. My mother, who never liked playing house, had wound up playing alone. It was the only game she knew.

She got the flu her last Christmas. Neither her fever nor her discomfort dissuaded her from hosting family dinner on Christmas Eve, but in the morning, her temperature spiked. She was sick for two weeks, and afterward, she was changed: fragile, aged, weakened, though she didn't complain or alter her routines. She died like a duchess at noon on the 12th of January, lying in bed waiting for her masseuse.

We disobeyed her. We didn't put her ashes out with the trash. On a cold, windy night at the end of January, we scattered them on the ground and plants and bushes in Parc Castell de l'Orenata, a park near my parents' house where, we told ourselves, she enjoyed walking, though really she thought taking walks was a waste of time and only did it to make us stop badgering her to follow the doctor's advice. In the morning, my aunt Carmen went to the park and reported to us that it was as white as if it had snowed.

It took me years to understand that my mother had let herself die. Maybe she decided to. She'd had enough of life, and she wasn't interested in living through her own decay. She was always a determined, resolute person: when she decided to do something, it got done.

Before she died, my brother Pablo made an hours-long video

of himself talking to her. I haven't dared to watch it yet. I'm not brave enough to hear her voice or see her face. I can imagine her on the sofa, wineglass in one hand and lit cigarette in the other, chatting animatedly with the camera. I asked Pablo if she talked about us, her kids, and he said, "Of course." I was afraid to hear what she'd said about me. What if she'd gone on about all the suffering and fear I put her through?

But Pablo said she'd mainly talked about the boys. "Not much about you or Blanca."

"What's 'not much?'"

In the video, what my mother says about me is this: "Clara? Clara's her sister's shadow."

I'm used to my life as a shadow now. My games are the difficult games of shadows, designed to halt the flow of a life that's impure, irrational, illogical; that pairs people and ideas that don't belong together, like me and my mother: she deserved another daughter, and I would have preferred another mother. When I was young, anyway. Not later, but by then it was too late.

Did I thank her? I'm not sure. I hope so, but I don't remember. I might not have. My family is stingy with our feelings. We get embarrassed. I imagine myself in a chair, my chair, in her living room. She's opposite me, reading the paper with her legs stretched out on the sofa.

"Mamá," I say. "I want to thank you for what you did for me. You saved my life."

She lowers the newspaper and looks at me over her glasses. She's uncomfortable. She's not ready for this Hollywood scene when our genre was supposed to be *destape*. "And I'd thank *you* not to put your feet on the table," she shoots back. "How many times do I have to ask?"

Sometimes I see two mothers, Sandra's and mine, sitting in the hard, slippery chairs in a hospital waiting room, anticipating news of their daughters. Both are afraid; both are in pain; both are hopeful, just a little, and just a little resigned. You have to prepare yourself for the worst in situations like that. Both are asking themselves what did I do wrong, what was my mistake, how could this have happened, how could my daughter—my daughter who was connected to me, who was part of me, who I birthed and nursed and held in a hospital like this one, who relied on me completely, who I took care of, who I kept safe—be here now, alone with her luck, behind those heavy metal ICU doors that I can't even go through? Both of them feel guilty. I'm not a mother, but I can imagine the injustice, these women telling themselves they're responsible for their daughters' fates, their missteps, their errors, even when the daughters in question are adults who struck out on their own long ago.

I came out of my coma. Sandra didn't. She plunged to the bottom of the pit I just dipped my feet in. When I woke up in the last hospital bed, needles and tubes in my arms and oxygen hose taped to my cheeks, I saw my mother watching at me and I felt a bittersweet, disappointed relief. I was here again. I had to start back up the mountain with my goddamn rock. I'd gotten so close to the place beyond the mountain, the place with no cares or fears. But that was a long time ago. I'm not interested in the pit anymore. I know it's waiting for me, and some day, any day, a day I don't expect it, the pit with its dark, murky, fathomless water will open before me and in it I'll see my own eyes.

www.ingramcontent.com/pod-product-compliance
Lightning Source LLC
Chambersburg PA
CBHW011648010726
47495CB00011B/2971

* 9 7 8 0 8 2 6 5 0 8 3 1 7 *